The Amish

Baker Caper

A WILLOW SPRINGS AMISH MYSTERY ROMANCE

Book 2

Tracy Fredrychowski

ISBN: 979-8-9906105-2-1(paperback)

ISBN: 979-8-9906105-1-4 (digital)

Published in South Carolina by The Tracer Group, LLC

https://tracyfredrychowski.com

"To my granddaughter, Taylor – my travel partner, marketing assistant, and mini-me. Your love for reading and the mystery surrounding you has been a constant source of inspiration. This story is for you, a fellow adventurer in both life and imagination. May you always embrace the wonders of a good mystery."

By Tracy Fredrychowski

AMISH OF LAWRENCE COUNTY SERIES

Secrets of Willow Springs – Book 1
Secrets of Willow Springs – Book 2
Secrets of Willow Springs – Book 3

APPLE BLOSSOM INN SERIES

Love Blooms at the Apple Blossom Inn
An Amish Christmas at the Apple Blossom Inn

NOVELLAS

The Amish Women of Lawrence County
An Amish Gift Worth Waiting For
The Orphan's Amish Christmas
An Amish Christmas Table: Love Beneath the Pine

THE AMISH WOMEN OF LAWRENCE COUNTY

Emma's Amish Faith Tested – Book 1
Rebecca's Amish Heart Restored – Book 2
Anna's Amish Fears Revealed – Book 3
Barbara's Amish Truth Exposed – Book 4
Allie's Amish Family Miracle – Book 5
Savannah's Amish Ties That Bind – Book 6

A WILLOW SPRINGS AMISH MYSTERY ROMANCE
The Amish Book Cellar – Book 1
The Amish Baker Caper – Book 2

www.tracyfredrychowski.com

Contents

A NOTE ABOUT AMISH VOCABULARY

The Amish language is called Pennsylvania Dutch and is usually spoken rather than written. The spelling of commonly used words varies from community to community throughout the United States and Canada. Even as I researched this book, some words' spelling changed within the same Amish community that inspired this story. In one case, spellings were debated between family members. Some of the terms may have slightly different spellings. Still, all came from my interactions with the Amish settlement near where I was raised in northwestern Pennsylvania.

While this book was modeled upon a small community in Lawrence County, this is a work of fiction. The names and characters are products of my imagination. They do not resemble any person, living or dead, or actual events in that community.

PROLOGUE

Thefts Rattle Amish Community
by Jonas Butler - The Buggy Crossing

Residents of Willow Springs are shaken by a recent string of thefts disrupting their peaceful community. The crimes, which began last week, have targeted prominent businesses and members of the New Order Fellowship Church, leaving residents scrambling for answers.

The thefts, including the disappearance of valuable items, have sown discord in the once-tranquil Amish community. Church leaders are urging members to take extra precautions to protect their belongings.

Local baker Ruthie Mast was among the

first to discover her treasured recipe box missing. "I can't understand why anyone would take such a personal item. It holds no monetary value," she remarked. "Some of the recipes are over 100 years old, handed down to me by my mother and grandmother."

Detective Powers from the Willow Springs Police Department has launched an investigation but has yet to identify any suspects. "We are treating this series of crimes with the utmost seriousness," Powers stated. "Our priority is to ensure the safety and security of all residents throughout Willow Springs."

The sudden wave of strange events has sparked speculation within the community. Some members are concerned about an outsider targeting the Amish, while others fear the crimes may be the work of someone within their midst, straining relations among neighbors.

In the wake of the thefts, residents are urged to remain vigilant and report any suspicious activity. Despite the challenges, there's hope that the perpetrators will be brought to justice and peace will be restored to Willow Springs.

CHAPTER 1

April had arrived in Northwestern Pennsylvania, breathing new life into Willow Springs. The crisp spring air carried the scent of blooming flowers and freshly tilled soil. Along Main Street, businesses stirred to activity, their doors swinging open, enjoying the unseasonably warm temperatures. Towering maple trees lined the street, embracing the subtle transition of new growth as tulips and daffodils peeked through the earth, adding a splash of color to the scene.

The sounds of birds chirping and the distant hum of tractors working the fields mixed with the rhythmic clinking of shop signs swaying in the breeze. The chatter of townsfolk greeting one another and the occasional laughter of children playing in the park added a lively soundtrack to the morning.

The sidewalk, cool and slightly damp from the morning dew, contrasted with the warmth of the sun that began to filter through the window of The Amish Bakery.

Ruthie Mast stood behind the counter of her beloved bakery, kneading dough with practiced hands as the scent of lemon and sugar lingered in the air. Her collection of mismatched tables and chairs and the full case of pastries waited patiently to be enjoyed by patrons.

A ray of sun warmed Ruthie's face as she opened the door and flipped over the open sign. The comforting aroma of warm bread and sweet treats escaped the door, in hopes of inviting customers inside.

Hilda Hiltey stepped into the bakery, her presence immediately noticeable not just by her girth, but by the faint, musty smell that seemed to follow her everywhere.

"Hello, Hilda," Ruthie greeted, forcing a smile.

Hilda didn't return her greeting. "I thought I'd stop by for something to curb my appetite as I wait for the bank to open."

With a knowing nod, Ruthie continued to arrange the pastries. "I hope it's not too busy for you. Bank business on Monday morning can be a hassle."

Hilda waved a dismissive hand. "Oh, I don't mind. Just some business with the bank manager. I like to get things done early." She stepped closer to the counter, her eyes wandering over the neatly arranged goods before settling on the old wooden recipe box perched on the corner of the counter.

"That's a lovely recipe box," Hilda remarked, her tone casual, but her eyes lingering on the intricate pinwheel design etched into the wood. "It looks like it's been around for a while."

Ruthie glanced at the box, a fond smile tugging at her lips. "*Jah*, it was my mother's. It's one of my most treasured possessions."

"I can see why you cherish it. Well, I'll take a couple of cinnamon rolls." Hilda's fingers tapped on the counter as if rushing Ruthie to fill her order quickly. "Family heirlooms are precious, aren't they? They hold so many memories."

Ruthie caught a whiff of the musty smell again, her nose wrinkling slightly. "They do. This box contains all our secret family recipes. It's like a piece of our history."

Hilda's smile seemed forced as Ruthie watched her glance over her shoulder.

Ruthie quickly packed the order, handing it over with a polite nod. "Here you go. Enjoy."

Hilda left without a word, and Ruthie turned back to her work, trying to shake off the lingering discomfort of the older woman who always seemed to be carrying a chip on her shoulder about something.

She had just completed her famous lemon, chocolate, apple, and raspberry fry pies. Unlike the typical store-bought fillings other Amish bakers used, her homemade filling recipes made her bakery incredibly successful among her *Englisch* customers.

Despite the inviting welcome to a new day, Ruthie couldn't shake the melancholy that dawdled within her after learning about another friend's upcoming marriage. As she worked, her mind wandered to the ache of loneliness that troubled her heart lately.

In an Amish community like Willow Springs, where marriage was highly valued, being single felt like a mark of failure. Eligible suitors were few and far between, and her abrupt personality scared away what was left of them. She couldn't help but feel left behind as she watched her friends pair off and start families.

The joyful chatter about weddings and children only deepened her sense of isolation. Ruthie longed for companionship but feared her sharp tongue and need for control made her unlovable. With each grasp of dough that she kneaded, it seemed to press her further into the realization that, in a place where marriage was a milestone, she was standing still, unable to move forward.

Lost in her thoughts, Ruthie barely noticed the familiar figure of her best friend, Lydia Troyer, owner of the Book Cellar, standing at the counter. The rich aroma of yeast from rising dough mingled with the scent of lemon and sugar infused the air with the sweetness of spring.

Lydia's gentle smile and chestnut hair, tucked tightly under her pressed white kapp, greeted her with a warm hello. "*Goot meiya*, Ruthie." Lydia lifted her nose, breathing deeply, and moaned, "It smells wonderful in here—like heaven on earth. It reminds me of the lemon verbena sprouting up in my garden."

Ruthie managed a small smile in return, grateful for the distraction her friend provided. "Good morning, Lydia."

Lydia approached the bakery case, her eyes scanning the array of baked goods. Ruthie let out a small sigh, her shoulders sagging. Lydia moved closer, a troubled look crossing her face. "You seem a bit down this morning. Is everything alright?"

Ruthie covered the dough to rise, wiped her hands on a towel, and leaned against the butcher block worktable. "Oh, it's nothing, really."

Lydia frowned, not convinced. "Come now, you're always

quick to share what's on your mind. Why are you suddenly keeping your thoughts to yourself?"

Ruthie hesitated, looking away. "I just don't want to bother you with my worries."

"Bother me? That's what friends are for. You know I'm here for you, always. Please, talk to me. What has you looking so down in the mouth today?"

Ruthie sighed again, deeper this time. "It's just… I don't think I'll ever find anyone to share life with." She paused, then continued, her voice etched with sadness. "I hate feeling like this, but I must admit I'm a little jealous of you and the others who are pairing off to start a life of their own. When will it be my turn?"

Lydia's eyes softened with concern. "You can't give up hope. There's someone out there for you… just watch and see."

Ruthie straightened, a sharp edge returning to her voice. "Hope? I've had my share of hope. It's time I face reality. I'm twenty-nine, practically an old maid by our standards. Maybe it's time I accept that I'm not meant to be married."

Lydia shook her head, refusing to accept Ruthie's defeatist attitude. "That's not true. You're strong and independent, and you know what you want. Those aren't bad qualities."

Ruthie snorted, crossing her arms. "Tell that to the men who can't handle a woman with a mind of her own. Face it, Lydia, I'm too set in my ways. Better to accept it now than keep hoping for something that will never happen."

Lydia reached across the counter and squeezed Ruthie's hand. "You deserve happiness. Don't let fear and doubt steal that from you."

Ruthie's resolution softened, but only slightly. "Maybe. But until then, I've got a bakery to run. No use crying over what I can't change."

Lydia moved to the coffee station and poured them a fresh cup as Ruthie retrieved two lemon fry pies from the case and joined her at a table under the front window.

"I understand," Lydia inserted softly. "I can only imagine how hard it is to stand back and watch others find love while you're still searching for your own." Lydia took a sip from her mug. "Love can find you in the most ordinary circumstances if you step out of *Gott's* way and let Him guide your path."

Ruthie scoffed, her bold personality shining through. "Step out of *Gott's* way? Please, I've practically built a highway for Him to send someone my way. But no one within twenty miles of this place catches my eye." She leaned her chin into the palm of her hand and groaned. "No one I'd even consider for a husband, for sure and certain."

Lydia snickered, trying to lighten the mood. "There are plenty of men to choose from. Could it be your expectations are too high?"

Ruthie straightened, a defiant flash in her eye. "Expectations? Lydia, I don't think wanting a man who can hold an actual conversation is asking too much. Most of them either grunt or stare at their boots when I talk. And don't get me started on the ones who think a woman's place is just in the kitchen."

Lydia smiled, shaking her head.

Ruthie's boldness softened to reveal a deeper layer. "I know my place as an Amish wife, really, I do. But I also have dreams that don't include giving up my bakery to raise a family. I want to do both. I need a man who understands and supports it. Is that too much to ask?"

Lydia's face turned serious, her eyes bursting with understanding. "No, it's not too much to ask. As long as you understand, it's going to take a special kind of man to concede to your wants and desires."

Ruthie shrugged, her boldness returning. "Maybe. But until

that special kind of man shows up, I'll keep running this bakery and living my life. I'm not going to settle for anything less than what I deserve."

Lydia took a sip from her mug before adding, "You're hardly ready for a permanent membership into the single girl's club."

Ruthie smirked. "I'm not going to say I haven't considered joining the Good Apple Girls Club a time or two."

Lydia crossed her legs, leaned back, and paused, thoughtfully considering Ruthie's options. "What about Jacob Kauffman? He's a hardworking farmer with a good heart."

Ruthie scoffed, her frustration bubbling to the surface. "Jacob? Please. He's as dull as dishwater. I need someone with more to offer in a conversation than an occasional grunt."

Ruthie snickered. "Have you ever heard him speak more than one-word answers to anyone? I know I talk a lot, but he doesn't talk at all!"

Lydia frowned at Ruthie's dismissive pitch. "Well, what about Samuel Glick? He's a skilled carpenter and could provide you with a good home."

Ruthie rolled her eyes, shaking her head in disbelief. "Samuel? He's too preoccupied with his construction business to even notice a woman. And besides, he's too much like his father. His father might be a good businessman, but as far as I can tell, he's not very good when it comes to family matters. I need someone who can balance both."

Lydia shrugged. "True, but Samuel is dependable. Didn't he build new shelves for you?"

Ruthie's head tilted as she nodded in thought. "*Jah*. He actually spent some time admiring my old recipe box. He mentioned the carving etched in the lid had to be done by an experienced woodcarver."

Lydia gave Ruthie a sympathetic look. "You've got high standards, and that's not a bad thing. But maybe you need to give someone a chance to surprise you."

Ruthie leaned back, a determined look in her eye. "Maybe." Lydia chuckled. "And that's why I like you. You're determined, and you know what you want. Just remember to keep your heart open along the way."

A small smile played on Ruthie's lips. "We'll see, Lydia. We'll see."

As Ruthie and Lydia continued their conversation, a sudden commotion outside drew their attention. Startled, they exchanged worried glances before rushing to the door to investigate.

The once peaceful morning buzzed with tension as shouts crammed the air. Two men sprinted past them down Main Street, their faces obscured by dark fabric. Behind them, the security guard from the bank pursued, the glint of his badge catching the sunlight. And right on his heels was a young Amish man whose broad shoulders and wind-blown hair left Ruthie with an odd sensation. Fear gripped her as she watched the scene unfold. "Lydia, what's happening?"

Lydia shook her head, her voice barely above a whisper. "I don't know, but we should stay back. That's the bank guard. I'm almost certain of it." Looking down toward the bank, nothing seemed amiss, and within seconds, more merchants appeared on the street, one exclaiming that someone had tried to rob the bank.

They stood frozen; their attention drawn to the chaos unfolding in the street. Ruthie leaned into Lydia. "Did you catch who that other man was?"

"I'm not sure, but it looked like the new owner of the buggy shop, Isaiah King. Aaron and I stopped there yesterday to welcome him to the community."

They watched as the four men disappeared in the alley

between a gap in the century-old brick buildings that lined the street. Neither dared to breathe as they followed a group of onlookers to the alley. Off in the distance, sirens rang as a police cruiser sped by, stopping in front of the bank.

When they saw nothing but a stray cat dart between them, Ruthie and Lydia stepped back to let a pair of uniformed officers run by. Suddenly, a loud crash echoed from somewhere down the street, and Ruthie's and Lydia's heads whipped around in unison, their eyes wide in alarm. "What was that?" Lydia exclaimed, her voice trembling in fear.

Ruthie's heart hammered in her chest as she exchanged a worried glance with Lydia. Without hesitation, they rushed back toward the bakery, their senses on high alert. Dread nibbled at Ruthie's stomach. She feared what they might find as they followed the sound back inside the bakery.

As they crossed the threshold, Ruthie's worst fears were confirmed. The once tidy bake shop lay in shambles. The glass case had been smashed, and the bakery rack turned over, spilling warm baked goods all over the floor. But the most devastating sight was the empty space where Ruthie's treasured recipe box should have been.

The old wooden box, with its intricately carved pinwheel

quilt pattern. The carvings were not just decorative; they held a sense of history and tradition, with each groove and swirl telling a story. The box had always sat proudly on the counter, a part of her deceased mother she treasured and the heart of her baking secrets. Now it was gone, leaving an aching void in its place.

Lydia gasped, her hand flying to her mouth. "Oh, Ruthie, who would do such a thing?"

Ruthie grasped her chest, her breath labored. She reached out a trembling hand to touch the empty spot as if hoping the box would somehow reappear. "This... this was my connection to my mother. Those recipes... they're irreplaceable."

***

Isaiah King stood back and surveyed the old buggy shop he had just purchased in Willow Springs. The building was in dire need of repairs, but it had always been his dream to own his own shop. Moving from Willow Brook to Willow Springs was his chance to start anew and perhaps find a woman who would accept him for who he was, quirks and all.

He knew his constant chattering and jittery tendencies, signs of his attention-deficit/hyperactivity disorder (ADHD), had put off many women in his old community. But here, he prayed things would be different. Repairing buggies kept his hands busy, and his mind focused, something other jobs failed to do. He pulled out a notepad and started making a list of necessary repairs and upgrades.

"Gotta build a sturdy new workbench," he muttered, tapping his pen against the notepad. His fingers twitched, a nervous habit he couldn't quite control. He glanced at the drafty walls. "Need to add insulation, new walls. Can't work in a freezer come winter." Squinting at the dim corners of the shop, he noted, "Better lighting, for sure. Can't fix what I can't see."

His eyes darted around at the clutter. "Shelves, racks, pegboards... Gotta keep things organized." Organization was always a challenge, but he was determined to improve.

Shuffling his feet on the uneven floor, he mumbled, "Fix the flooring. Safety first." The old windows rattled in their frames. "New windows. Need to keep the cold out and let the light in."

He measured the space in the corner. "A wood stove or something. Need heat for the winter." Finally, looking at the exterior, he sighed, "Paint and seal everything. Protect it from the elements."

Isaiah meticulously made his list, going over it repeatedly, afraid he might forget something important. His constant need to check and recheck was a habit he wished he could break, but it provided him a sense of control over his chaotic mind. He thought about his tics—constant chattering, fidgeting with his shirt collar, difficulty focusing, impulsivity, restlessness, organizational challenges, and repetitive checking. He tried to control these as best as possible, hoping not to let people see his struggles.

Isaiah knew that managing his ADHD required more than just willpower. Keeping sugary treats out of his diet, adding lots of fresh fruits and vegetables, and staying away from carbs helped him manage the severity of his symptoms. Living on his own and away from his mother's desserts seemed to be helping, but the location of his buggy shop right behind the bakery made it difficult. The delicate smells coming from the shop kept his mind focused on the treats he missed so dearly.

He picked up the almost empty bottle of all-natural tincture the Amish herbal lady had made for him and made a note to stop and buy more. He needed to do everything he could to keep his symptoms under control if he wanted to make a fresh start.

He paused, looking around the shop and back to his growing to-do list. This was his chance for a fresh start, where no one knew him or his history. Here, he could rebuild not just the buggy shop but his life. He was resolved to keep his quirky inclinations hidden, not wanting his new community to judge him too harshly.

Isaiah tucked his list in his pocket and headed to the bank, eager to open a new account. He locked the small apartment tucked in the back of the buggy shop and stepped out into the bright morning. He felt blessed to find a business that was already established to accommodate a single man. He hoped he didn't have to live there forever and had high hopes of buying a house someday. For now, as he built his business and became a working member of his new community, it was perfect.

As he walked through the alley leading to Main Street and the bank, the scent of the bakery filled the air. Stopping to look down Main Street to the sign for *The Amish Baker*, he felt drawn to stop in to admire the baked goods, even though he had no plans on making a purchase. But at the last minute, he turned toward the bank, fighting the urge to give in to the sweet temptation.

Just as he stepped up to the bank doors, they flew open, and two men with their faces covered by ski masks barreled out, shoving Isaiah aside. He stumbled and nearly fell, catching himself on the doorframe. The bank security guard was right behind them. There was no doubt the men had tried to rob the bank, and without thinking twice, Isaiah sprinted after them, his heart pounding.

The guard was already running after them, but his age and shorter stride left him lagging. With his longer legs, Isaiah quickly closed the distance and passed the guard. The two men dashed into the alley, their footsteps echoing off the brick walls.

Isaiah saw the flash of a crowbar in one of the men's hands, and his determination to help surged. He had to catch them before they hurt someone. He took off, giving no thought to how the leaders of his new church would react to his need to help.

As they reached the end of the alley, the two men jumped into an old blue car. He managed to grab the door handle, but the car jerked forward, dragging him a few feet before he lost his grip and fell to the ground. He rolled and scrambled to his feet, reaching out to the security guard, who had finally caught up.

"Did you get the license plate?" the guard wheezed, clutching his chest.

"It didn't have one, as far as I could tell," Isaiah panted as the car sped away.

Isaiah's ADHD often made him hyper-focused during crises, allowing him to think clearly and respond quickly during intense situations.

Moments later, two police officers came running up.

"What's your name, son?"

"Isaiah King," he replied, glancing nervously at the guard.

"Did you get the license plate number?"

Isaiah shook his head.

He had wanted a fresh start in Willow Springs but hadn't expected it to begin like this.

CHAPTER 2

After a long sigh, Isaiah felt aggravated that he had to make another run for supplies. He was heading to the Mercantile when he remembered what the post office clerk told him that morning. "Isaiah, we had a mix-up, and one of your packages was delivered to the bakery by mistake."

He needed those tools to finish the workbench he was working on. A little detour shouldn't bother him so much, but he knew how those unexpected changes to his schedule often disturbed him for hours. He briskly walked toward the bakery.

As he stepped inside, the smell of freshly baked bread and pastries enveloped him. The young woman behind the counter seemed to be busy arranging cookies in clear containers and barely acknowledged his arrival.

Isaiah approached the counter, noticing the cleanliness of the place. His own hands were grubby from working on the shop, and he hesitated for a moment before speaking. "Excuse me, I'm Isaiah King. The post office said a package meant for me was delivered here by mistake."

Ruthie's eyes narrowed slightly at the sight of his hands leaving smudges on her clean counter. She forced a polite smile, though her eyes remained hard. "Why would I have your package?"

Isaiah, immediately put off by her sharp reply, added, "The post office made an error. Can you please check?"

Ruthie sighed heavily, wiping her hands on a towel. "Fine. Just a moment." She searched behind the counter and found the package, handing it over to him. "Here. Maybe you should give them the correct address next time."

Isaiah, irritated by her tone and the way she seemed to look down on him, retorted, "It wasn't my fault. It has the correct address. See." He held out the package and pointed to the smudged address. "Maybe if you checked your deliveries, you could have saved us both the inconvenience."

Ruthie's eyes flashed with annoyance. "I don't have time to check every package the minute it arrives. As you can see, I'm trying to run a business here."

Isaiah took the package, muttering something about her tone, while Ruthie fumed over his lack of respect and the grubby marks left on her counter.

Isaiah left, but he couldn't shake the feeling that there was something more bothering the bakery owner than just a misplaced package. As he walked out the door, he shamed himself for not setting the nature of their first meeting better.

He had hoped to purchase some baked goods for his waiting customers to enjoy, hoping the bake shop would offer a slight discount for a steady order. Now, he worried that he had ruined that chance with his gruff demeanor.

***

No sooner had Isaiah left than Annie Hostetler, who worked next door at her parents' Quilt Market, walked in. "Who was that?" she asked, holding the door open and looking down the street at Isaiah's disappearing form.

"Isaiah King. He walked in here like he owned the place, leaving marks all over my counter and demanding I drop everything I was doing to look for a misdelivered package!"

Annie smiled calmly. "Ruthie, come now, I'm sure it wasn't that bad. You need to be a tad more friendly with newcomers."

Ruthie huffed. "Friendly? He needs to learn some manners

instead of coming in here and demanding I drop everything. And look at the mess he left on the counter!"

Annie leaned forward, her voice gentle. "Sounds like you're being a bit too harsh. He's new here and probably trying to find his footing. It doesn't sound like you offered him much of a welcome."

Ruthie exhaled, her frustration ebbing slightly. "Maybe you're right. I guess I let my frustration over the break-in and this huge order get in the way of being cordial."

As Ruthie and Annie continued their conversation, Ruthie couldn't help but recall his sandy blond hair and how it curled up around the brim of his straw hat. And those eyes… crystal blue if there was a crystal that color, that's what she dreamed the shade would be—features she'd never noticed on a man before—kept resurfacing.

The brim of his hat, much wider than those of her *g'may*, instantly told her he was new to Willow Springs. So new that he hadn't had a chance to change church membership and adhere to the *Ordnung* rules.

Annie closed the door and moved to the counter. "Keep an open mind. Sometimes, first impressions can be misleading. You never know what someone is dealing with. He could have been in a hurry or really needed whatever was in that package. Who knows what was on his mind?"

Ruthie dipped her head in acknowledgment, her thoughts drifting back to Isaiah's guarded expression. "I suppose. But he better not leave grubby marks on my counter again."

Annie chuckled, the sound lightening the mood. "Just remember, everyone deserves a little grace and a welcoming smile."

Ruthie smiled, albeit reluctantly. "Alright, I'll try to be more understanding next time… if there's even a next time."

As Ruthie and Annie continued their conversation, Ruthie couldn't help replaying the image of him fussing with his collar during their brief encounter. He was nervous, alright… which made her question his true intentions. Shaking her head to clear out the crazy thoughts, she turned her attention back to Annie. "Did you need something?"

"*Jah. Mamm* wants two loaves of bread. We've been so busy this week that we haven't had time to bake."

The small bell above the bakery door jingled, announcing Detective Powers's arrival just as Ruthie handed Annie her change and bread order.

Detective Powers was a tall man with a stern face softened

by kind eyes, known for his thoroughness and dedication to keeping Willow Springs safe.

"Good morning, Detective," Ruthie greeted him, trying to keep her voice steady despite the turmoil she felt inside. The theft of her recipe box still weighed heavily on her mind, and seeing the detective brought it all rushing back.

"Morning, Ruthie," Detective Powers replied, his voice gentle but authoritative. "I came to ask you a few questions about the break-in." He pulled out a small notepad and a pen. "Can you tell me if there's any reason you can think of why someone would target your bakery?"

"I can't think of why anyone would want to tip over my cases or take my recipe box, except maybe for the recipes themselves."

Detective Powers jotted down notes, his brow furrowing in concentration. "Have you seen anyone acting suspiciously around the bakery recently? Any new customers or people lingering around?"

Ruthie thought for a moment, shaking her head. "No one comes to mind immediately. Everyone who comes in is usually here for the pastries or to chat. Nothing out of the ordinary."

The detective nodded, flipping a page in his notepad. "And

the break-in itself, was there anything unusual about it? Any signs that might suggest who did it?"

A sigh escaped Ruthie as the memory of the wrecked bakery was still fresh. "The glass case was smashed, and the bakery rack was turned over. It seemed like whoever did it was looking for something specific, but the recipe box was the only thing taken."

Detective Powers looked thoughtful, tapping his pen against the notepad. "It's strange. Recipe boxes don't typically hold much monetary value, but the recipes inside could be worth something to the right person. I'll need to look into this further."

He shut his notebook and slipped it back into his pocket. "I'll keep you updated on any developments. In the meantime, if you think of anything else, no matter how small, please let me know."

With a reassuring nod, Ruthie felt a glimmer of hope. "Thank you, Detective. I just want to get it back. It means everything to me."

***

Ruthie was finishing wiping down the counter and getting

ready to close for the day when a man she had never seen before walked into the bakery. His clothes were neat but slightly worn, and his hair was unkempt, giving him a disheveled appearance. He looked around the shop with an almost unnerving interest, his eyes darting from the baked goods to her and back to the door.

Ruthie offered him a polite smile. "Hello. How can I help you today?"

The man hesitated; his gaze fixed on the display case. "Good afternoon. I was just wondering about your fried pies. They look delicious."

Ruthie's curiosity piqued. "Thank you. They're quite popular. Would you like to try one?"

The stranger seemed to ponder this for a moment before shaking his head. "Are they fresh today?"

Ruthie tilted her head slightly, unsure of his intentions. "*Jah*, everything's made from scratch, and I only keep things a day or two before I replace them."

As Ruthie answered his questions, a few regular customers came in. The stranger stepped aside, letting them go ahead of him. Ruthie served them quickly, but her unease grew as she noticed the man lingering near the counter, his eyes never leaving the display case.

"Is there anything else you'd like to know?" Ruthie asked as she handed a bag of bread to one of the customers.

The man nodded; his interest undiminished. "What about the filling? Do you make that here too?"

Ruthie forced a smile, trying to maintain her composure. "Yes, I do. It's an old family recipe."

The last customer left, leaving Ruthie alone with the stranger. She purposely left the door open, a small comfort in case the man had other ideas.

He stepped closer to the counter, his voice dropping to a near whisper. "An old family recipe, huh? Must be quite a secret."

Ruthie felt a shiver run down her spine. "It is. Is there something specific you're looking for?"

The man shrugged, a strange smile playing on his lips. "Just curious. It's been a long time since I had an authentic fry pie, and the cashier at the Mercantile recommended your shop."

Ruthie's unease deepened. "We appreciate the recommendation. Is there something you'd like to try?"

The man shook his head again. "Not today. I was wondering about the thefts I read about in the newspaper. Were any other merchants targeted that day?"

Ruthie's heart skipped a beat. "I'm not sure. Why do you ask?"

The man smiled most peculiarly. "Just trying to get the full picture. It's interesting how someone would target an Amish bakery and nothing else."

With a nod of farewell, Ruthie was eager to end the conversation. "If there's nothing else, I have some work to get back to."

The man looked around the bakery one last time before stepping back. "I suppose that's all for now. Thank you for answering my questions, Ruthie."

Ruthie's breath caught. "How do you know my name?"
The man chuckled, but it was devoid of warmth. "I read it in the newspaper. Have a good day."

With that, he turned and walked out, leaving Ruthie standing behind the counter, her mind racing. She closed the door and locked it, her hands trembling slightly. Something was unsettling about the stranger, and she couldn't banish the feeling that his interest in her was more than just curiosity.

Ruthie made a mental note to mention the encounter to Lydia later. Something about the man's behavior didn't sit right with her, and she had an uncanny sensation she'd met him before.

***

Evert Miller exited the bakery, feeling Ruthie's uneasy stare lingering on his back. As he stepped out onto the sidewalk, he let out a slow breath, his eyes scanning the quaint town he used to call home. He pulled his worn baseball cap lower over his face and made his way down the street, blending into the surroundings as best as he could.

His mind raced with the information he had gathered. The bakery, with its delicious fry pies and the recent theft, was just a piece of the conundrum he was in. He reached into his pocket and pulled out a small, crumpled photograph, staring at it for a moment.

The picture was old and faded, showing a group of Amish children standing in front of a large barn. He traced his finger over one of the faces, a young girl with a stern look. He'd held on to the only picture he had of his childhood friends as if it was a lifeline to a time, he could no longer partake in.

"Ruthie Mast," he muttered under his breath. "You haven't

changed a bit."

He slipped the photograph back into his pocket and continued walking, his steps purposeful. He had been aching to return to Willow Springs for years, and the theft at the bakery was just what he needed to pick up where he left off years ago.

"Old family recipes. What do they have in common with the other clues I'd been following?" he muttered to himself, typing quickly on his phone. "Ruthie is cautious but not suspicious. She didn't recognize me."

He thought back to his conversation with Ruthie. Her guarded demeanor, the way she had tried to keep him at arm's length, and the way she left the door open—subtle signs that she didn't trust easily.

He approached a small bench near the park in the center of town and sat down, pulling out a notebook from his coat pocket. Flipping through the pages, he found the section where he had meticulously documented every detail of what information he had gathered thus far. Each entry had a date, a location, and a possible hint to the puzzle he'd been trying to solve for over fifteen years.

"The recipe box," he whispered to himself, tapping his pen against the paper. "Why would someone want that? What clue did it hold to the next?"

He scribbled a few notes in his book, underlining key phrases: "Old family recipe," "Ingredients," and "Small wooden box." There was something about those recipes, something that made them valuable enough to steal. But was it the recipes? Or something else that held an old family secret?

A passing couple gave him a curious glance, and he quickly closed his notebook, slipping it back into his coat. He stood up and began walking again, heading towards the outskirts of town. He had to find out more about Ruthie and her family and if they had anything in common with his own.

There was a connection here, something that linked her to his family. One thing he knew for sure was that Ruthie's bakery was just the first in a series of clues.

He turned down a side street, heading toward a small motel he was staying at. The room was cluttered with papers, maps, and photographs. He pushed open the door and sat at the small desk, spreading out his notes in front of him.

He picked up a photograph of Ruthie's bakery, taken from a distance. And another of the old buggy shop behind it. Isaiah King, the new owner, held a piece to the puzzle—he was sure of it. He made a mental note to watch his cousin more closely.

Evert leaned back in his chair, staring at the photographs and notes scattered across the desk. He had to be careful. His interest in the bakery theft couldn't draw too much attention. He needed to blend in, keep asking questions, and piece together the mystery without revealing too much about his own motives.

Evert sat alone in the dim light of his rented room; the curtains drawn tight to keep prying eyes out. The silence was heavy, broken only by two people arguing in the room next door. He reached into his pocket and pulled out the crumpled photograph he had been carrying for years. The image, worn and faded, connected him to a past he couldn't ignore a minute longer.

His eyes lingered on the faces, memories of a simpler time flooding back. Noah, Ruthie, and Annie had been his childhood friends. They had shared laughs, secrets, and countless hours of play. But that was some fifteen years ago before he had left the Amish community and chosen a different path. He doubted they'd even remember him now.

Evert's gaze focused on the young Ruthie in the photograph. Her stern expression and determined eyes were just as he remembered. He traced a finger over her face, his mind vying with plans and possibilities. The secret camera he'd stolen from the Mercantile was the first time he felt the adrenaline rush of crime.

"You're the key to all this," he whispered. "And I'm going to find out why before harm comes to you or your family." He couldn't afford to let sentimentality cloud his judgment.

He folded the photograph carefully and slipped it back into his pocket. He stood up, pacing the small room as he thought about his next move. He needed to be careful, to stay one step ahead of anyone who might get in his way.

The thought of someone using Ruthie, Noah, and Annie as pawns in their game troubled him. They were just means to an end, pieces on a chessboard that they could move at will. His time among the English had taught him that you had to be ruthless to get ahead, and the men who were after him had no qualms about using anyone to achieve their goals.

Evert's lips curled into a cold smile as he thought about the coming days. He had waited long enough, and now it was time to act. He would uncover the secrets of the past and claim the treasure that was rightfully his family's.

As he pondered his next move, he couldn't help but think back to the people who might be watching him. He had to remain vigilant. After all, he had a past in Willow Springs, one that not everyone had forgotten. The old photo, and his own return to this town, it all painted a picture that could easily cast suspicion on him if he wasn't careful.

Evert had been staying one step ahead of his enemies for years. But all the clues were leading him back to his hometown, and he came out of hiding, hoping to find a quick way to settle up with those who'd do anything to get what they were owed.

Evert began plotting his next move. He knew Willow Springs held secrets, and he was driven to uncover them, no matter what it took. As long as he stayed one step ahead of the suspicions that were bound to arise, he might succeed in putting an end to the whole crazy mess his family had made.

***

Still shaken from her brief encounter with the strange man who showed up at the bakery, Ruthie decided to stop by Lydia and Aaron Troyer's on her way home.

The unsettling customer left her with a nagging feeling of familiarity she couldn't shake. She hoped Aaron and Lydia, good friends with Detective Lewis Powers, might have heard some news about the ongoing investigation. She also wanted to mention the strange visitor who had left her so on edge.

As she approached the Troyer's cozy farmhouse, the smells of an evening meal wafted through the air. Ruthie took a deep breath, trying to steady her nerves before speaking through the screen door. Yankee, the brown lab, was lounging on the porch and perked up at the sight of her.

"Hey, Yankee!" Ruthie greeted the dog warmly, bending down to scratch him behind his ears. He wagged his tail enthusiastically, giving Ruthie a comforting nudge.

"Ruthie! What a pleasant surprise," Lydia greeted her with a warm smile, opening the door wide. "Come in, come in. We were just having dinner."

"Ruthie! Aunt Ruthie!" Mattie Rose and Julia, Lydia and Aaron's daughters, came running from the front room, their faces lighting up with excitement. They each gave Ruthie a hug, their enthusiasm bringing a genuine smile to her face.

"Thank you," Ruthie said, stepping inside.

"Have a seat." Lydia invited as she pointed to a seat between the girls.

"I don't want to intrude," Ruthie began, but Lydia was already guiding her to a chair at the table and pulling another plate from the cupboard.

Ruthie smiled weakly. "I appreciate it. I wanted to talk to you both about something."

Aaron raised an eyebrow. "Is everything alright?" Ruthie exhaled a sigh as the events of the day weighed heavily on her mind. "I had a stranger at the bakery just before closing. A man I've never seen before came in, asking odd questions about my fry pies and my recipe box. He kept looking toward the door like he was nervous about something. He lingered even after all the other customers had left."

Lydia and Aaron exchanged concerned glances. "What did he look like?" Aaron asked, his voice taking on a more serious sound.

"He was tall, with unkempt hair and a worn baseball cap. His clothes were neat but looked like they had seen better days. He seemed... familiar, but I couldn't place him," Ruthie explained, her brow furrowing. "And he was shifty. The way he kept glancing at the door made me uncomfortable."

"Did he say anything that stood out to you?" Lydia asked gently.

"He mentioned reading about the theft in the newspaper and asked if any other merchants were targeted that day," Ruthie said, her voice trembling slightly. "He knew my name from the article, but it felt like more than just casual curiosity. I have a feeling English wasn't his first language. His words were precise... almost forced."

Aaron nodded thoughtfully. "It sounds suspicious. I'll make sure to mention it to Lewis when I see him, but I don't think the police department is spending much time on this case anymore. The attempted bank robbery has them working harder to look for the culprits." Aaron spread butter onto a slice of bread and asked, "Did he leave anything behind, or do anything else that seemed unusual?"

Ruthie shook her head. "No, he just kept letting people go ahead of him, and when he finally spoke to me, he seemed more interested in the box than in making a purchase. There was an odd sensation like I'd met him before, but I can't remember where."

Lydia reached out and squeezed Ruthie's hand. "You did the right thing by coming here. We'll make sure Detective Powers knows about this."

Ruthie straightened her shoulders, her bold spirit shining through. "I'm not going to let this theft bother me. I'll figure out what's going on and get to the bottom of it. The biggest thing is I'm not sure I remember all the recipes by heart. That worries me."

They all took a minute to bow their heads and bless the food before Ruthie continued. "Oh, and I met Isaiah King," Ruthie added, her pitch turning sharp. "He wasn't anything like you described. He was rude and impatient. He was also so nervous and shifty; it made me just as uncomfortable as the guy this afternoon."

Lydia looked surprised. "Really? He seemed nice when Aaron and I met him. Maybe he was having a bad day?"

Ruthie shook her head. "The whole day has been a series of unsettling occurrences."

As they shared a meal and continued discussing the day's events, Ruthie felt a sense of relief. She was grateful for friends like Lydia and Aaron, who provided comfort and support during such uncertain times. Yet the mystery of the strange man and the missing recipe box lingered in her mind, a puzzle she was determined to solve.

CHAPTER 3

Against her better judgment, Ruthie found herself driving her buggy up to Isaiah King's buggy shop after she locked up the bakery for the day. The foot brake had been giving her problems for a few days, and it was clear she needed professional help.

She reluctantly admitted that Isaiah was the best option available. As she approached the shop, the sound of metal clinking and tools clattering filled the air. Isaiah was busy at work, his back turned to her.

She took a full breath and called out, "Isaiah King?"
Isaiah turned around, a look of surprise flashing across his face before he quickly composed himself. "*Jah*?"

Ruthie bit her lip, still wary of his previous behavior. "My buggy's foot brake isn't working right. Can you look at it?"

Isaiah nodded, wiping his hands on a rag as he approached her buggy. "Of course. Let's see what we've got here."

Ruthie began to explain how the brake kept sticking, and she couldn't help but observe him adjusting his collar repeatedly as she tried to explain the issue.

Isaiah had a sincere look on his face as he interrupted her. "I owe you an apology for the way I acted the other day."

Ruthie blinked, taken aback by his unexpected apology. She nodded slowly. "It's no problem."

Isaiah smiled, his eyes warm and genuine. "I've been a bit stressed with the move and getting this shop up and running. It's no excuse, but I hope you can understand."

Ruthie gave him a small smile in return. "I do. Moving and starting over can be overwhelming for sure and certain."

Isaiah adjusted his collar one last time before kneeling to inspect the brake. "You know, a foot brake is a critical component of a buggy. It operates by applying pressure to the brake shoes, which then press against the wheels to slow them down. If it's sticking, it could be due to dirt or wear in the mechanism. It's essential to have it working correctly for safety reasons, especially when going downhill or stopping suddenly."

Ruthie listened, trying to keep up with his constant chatter. She wasn't used to a man being so talkative, and it threw her off balance. Normally, she was the one carrying the conversation, but Isaiah's endless stream of words made her feel like she was playing catch-up.

"Really?" she said, trying to sound interested. "I didn't know that."

Isaiah gave an enthusiastic nod. "Oh yes, and did you know there are many different types of buggies? The design can vary greatly depending on the region and the specific needs of the community. It's quite fascinating when you think about it."

Ruthie tried to maintain her composure, but his nonstop talking and the constant collar adjustment made her uneasy. Was it just a nervous habit, or was it her presence making him fidgety? She took a step back, keeping her distance. "It sounds like you know a lot about buggy design."

Isaiah laughed, adjusting his collar once more. "I suppose I do. It's always been a passion of mine, and I've studied long and hard on the subject. Ask me anything about buggies, and I'll know the answer. It's been a good way to keep my mind busy, you know?"

Ruthie nodded, though she still felt a bit wary. "I see."

Isaiah's hands moved quickly, and within minutes, he had the brake adjusted. "There, that should do it. Give it a try."

Ruthie climbed into the buggy and tested the brake. It

worked perfectly. She looked down at Isaiah, who was watching her expectantly, his fingers still fidgeting with his collar. "Thank you. It seems to be working now."

Isaiah grinned, his hands finally stilling. "I'm glad I could help. If you ever need anything else, don't hesitate to ask."

Ruthie reached into her pocketbook, pulling out some money. "How much do I owe you?"

Isaiah shook his head, holding up his hands. "Nothing. I owe you for my rude behavior the other day. Consider it an apology."

Ruthie nodded, still cautious, but feeling a bit more at ease. "I will. Thank you again."

As she drove away, Ruthie couldn't help but think his apology and enthusiasm seemed genuine, but his nervous chatter and constant collar adjustment still left her questioning his odd behavior.

***

Just as Ruthie was about to put a tray of cookies in the oven, the bakery door swung open, and Lydia and Annie stepped inside, their faces flushed.

"Ruthie, have you heard what happened at the Quilt Market?" Annie asked, her voice trembling.

Ruthie placed the tray down and turned to face them. "No, what's going on?"

Annie stepped forward, her face reflecting the confusion and frustration of the previous night. "Someone broke in last night and the only thing my parents could figure out that had been taken was an old ledger recording all the quilts sold in 1980. We're stumped at what value the old ledger might have."

Ruthie's brow furrowed in confusion. "A ledger? That doesn't make any sense. Why would anyone steal that?"

Annie shook her head. "Detective Powers said the same thing. He doesn't think the two thefts are connected. He mentioned that the break-in here might be more about the recipes and less about the ledger."

Ruthie leaned against the counter, trying to make sense of it all. "It's just so strange. My recipe box and now an old quilt ledger. What's the connection?"

Annie shrugged. "Detective Powers suggested that someone might be trying to disrupt local businesses. But why target us? It's not like we're sitting on a treasure trove."

Ruthie thought for a moment. "Did the detective say

anything else?"

Contemplatively, Annie nodded. "He mentioned that he's investigating other angles too. He asked if we had seen anyone suspicious around the Quilt Market recently. But we couldn't think of anyone."

Ruthie bit her lip, her mind racing. "Do you think it could be someone from outside the community? Maybe someone who doesn't understand the value we place on these things?"

Annie considered this. "It's possible. But why go through the trouble of stealing something so specific? And how did they even know about the ledger?"

Ruthie sighed, her shoulders slumping. "I don't know. But we need to find out. Maybe we're missing something."

With a respectful nod, Lydia added, "Exactly."

Ruthie felt a chill run down her spine. "I saw two men on the street early this morning when I came in to start making bread. I'd never seen them before, and they were acting so strange I couldn't help but wonder what they were up to."

"What on earth could the recipe box and ledger have in common? Two items that hold no monetary value?" Lydia asked.

As they discussed the strange events, the door opened again, and Isaiah walked in. He hesitated for a moment, noticing the tense atmosphere.

"Ruthie, I wanted to talk to you about—" He paused, sensing it wasn't the right time. "Is everything alright?"

Ruthie gave him a brief smile. "You might want to hear this. We're talking about the break-in at the Quilt Market last night."

"A break-in? What happened?"

Annie quickly filled him in on the details. "Someone stole an old ledger from 1980. My parents can't figure out why anyone would want something so old and useless."

Isaiah's stare turned thoughtful. "That's strange. A recipe box and a ledger—neither seems valuable on the surface, but there must be something connecting them."

Lydia nodded. "That's what we were thinking. But what could it be?"

Isaiah rubbed his chin, his mind clearly racing. "Sometimes it's not the item itself but the information it holds. Maybe there's something in that ledger that points to something else."

Ruthie looked at him, intrigued despite her initial wariness. "What do you mean?"

Isaiah shrugged. "It's just a hunch, but what if the ledger contains records or notes that are important for some other reason?"

Annie's eyes lit up. "But how do we figure that out if the ledger is gone?"

Isaiah smiled. "We start by talking to people who might remember the ledger's contents. Maybe there are old records or memories that can help discover why someone would steal it."

Annie nodded. "My grandparents owned the quilt shop then and are quite elderly. I'm unsure if they will remember much, but we can ask."

She paused, then added, "You know, the collection of ledgers goes back almost a hundred years, and a quilt design is always embossed on the leather cover, according to the year's popular design. I can't help but wonder what design was etched on the stolen ledger."

Lydia headed to the door. "Well… I can't stand here all day trying to figure things out. I have a bookshop to open."

"I'll be sure to talk to my grandparents tonight," Annie said as she followed Lydia out the door.

Lydia and Annie left, and Isaiah and Ruthie were left alone in the bakery.

Isaiah shifted nervously, adjusting his collar. "I wanted to ask if you'd be willing to supply my shop with sweet treats for my customers."

"What did you have in mind?"

Thoughtfully, Isaiah nodded. "Just a little something to keep them happy and content while they wait on me to fix their buggy."

"Is this a one-time order, or do you want an ongoing order?

The way Ruthie asked him the simplest question in such a professional manner left him wanting to get to know her more. There was no doubt the way she carried herself left him intrigued. She wasn't like any young woman he'd ever known.

***

The bakery felt unusually quiet after the morning's discussions. Ruthie was deep in thought, trying to piece together the mystery, when the doorbell chimed again.

Samuel Glick stepped into the bakery, his presence filling the small shop. "Good afternoon, Ruthie," he greeted with a warm but conniving smile.

"Hello," Ruthie replied, wiping her hands on her apron.

"I heard about the break-in at the Quilt Market," Samuel said, his manner turning serious. "I've been thinking about your recipe box. I noticed it had a pinwheel design etched on it, right?"

Ruthie nodded slowly. "*Jah*, it did. Why?"

"Well," Samuel began, his tone careful, "can you remember any specific details about the design? Sometimes, these patterns have more significance than we realize."

Ruthie thought for a moment, trying to recall the details. "It was a traditional pinwheel design, I suppose. Nothing out of the ordinary."

Samuel's eyes seemed to light up with interest. "I'd like to help you replace that recipe box. I can make you a new one, perhaps even better than the old one. It might not be the same, but at least it will keep your recipes safe."

Ruthie felt a twinge of suspicion at his eagerness. "That's very kind of you, Samuel, but I don't want to bother you."

"It's no trouble at all," Samuel insisted. "Consider it a gesture of goodwill, but I would need you to sketch as much of the design as you can remember. I want to make it as close to the original as possible."

Ruthie forced a smile. "Thank you, Samuel. I'll think about it."

As Samuel left, Ruthie couldn't shake the feeling that there was more to his interest than he was letting on. While generous, his offer to make her a new recipe box seemed oddly timed and out of character to his self-absorbed personality.

***

The two men stood across the street from the Quilt Market, leaning on their car, their eyes fixed on the scene unfolding in front of them. The taller man, dressed in jeans and a t-shirt, scanned the area with a sharp gaze.

"If he's here, he'll show up," he muttered to his companion. The shorter man, whose clothes were slightly worn but clean, nodded in agreement. "Could be," he replied, his voice low and cautious.

The taller man glanced around nervously. "Do you think Miller knows we're on his trail?"

The taller man shrugged. "Hard to say. He's been lying low, but I'm certain he's here. He has connections to the Amish here. It only makes sense he'd come here if he was going to move."

The shorter man kicked at a loose pebble on the ground. "This place is too small for him to hide forever. If he's here, someone will have seen him."

The taller man nodded. "Agreed. We need to ask around, but carefully. We can't let anyone know we're looking for him. Especially not Miller. If he gets wind of us, he'll vanish again."

The shorter sighed in frustration. "We've been chasing him for years. It's high time we get what he owes us and leave this two-bit town. If I step over one more horse dropping or have to smell manure filled fields one more day, I think I'll puke."

The taller man's eyes narrowed as he glanced at the Quilt Market, where a small crowd was gathering. "Think anyone here knows anything?"

"Maybe," the shorter man replied. "This town isn't that big. Someone must have seen him." The shorter man adjusted his hat, a determined look in his eyes. "Alright. Let's split up and see what we can find out. Meet back here in an hour."

The taller man nodded. "Stay sharp. We're getting close. I can feel it."

As the two men moved away from the car and blended into the crowd, their mission was clear. Find Evert Miller and fast.

***

Ruthie decided to take a break from the bakery for a few

minutes. She flipped the closed sign and stepped outside. The cool spring air was a welcome relief from the hot bakery, and she began a leisurely walk around the block. As she rounded the corner, she saw Isaiah at his buggy shop, working on releasing a stubborn wheel. She stopped a few feet away, watching him from a distance.

Isaiah's focused glare and the way he expertly handled the tools intrigued her. She found herself wondering what had brought him to Willow Springs. She quickly shook off her thoughts and decided to take him some bakery samples instead.

With a quick breath, Ruthie squared her shoulders and returned to the bakery to prepare a small basket of her best treats. She filled it with a variety of fried pies, donuts, and cookies, all freshly made that morning. Once she was satisfied with the selection, she walked back to Isaiah's shop with purpose.

"Isaiah," she called out as she approached, holding up the basket with a smile. "I brought you some samples from the bakery. Thought you might like to try them to know what your customers might like."

Isaiah looked up, surprised, but quickly composed himself. "Don't eat sweets," he said abruptly, almost cutting her off.

Ruthie's smile faltered. "You don't eat sweets? At all?"

Isaiah shook his head as he continued with the heavy wheel. "Nope, sugars and carbs mess with me. It's hard for me to stay focused, and everything just spirals out of control if I eat too much. Thanks anyways."

Ruthie was taken aback by his rapid explanation. "I see. But don't you think it's important to at least sample the items you're planning to offer your customers?"

Isaiah didn't miss a beat. "I trust your reputation. I mean, everyone talks about how great your bakery is. I hear it all the time. Especially your lemon pies. And I've seen the lines outside your bakery. People love what you make. So, I don't need to try them to know they're good. Plus, if I even have a little bit, it could throw off my entire day, and then I'd be all over the place, and that's not good for anyone… trust me."

As Isaiah continued talking, Ruthie spotted Jedediah Weaver entering the shop behind him. The man waited patiently, but Isaiah was so engrossed in his explanation that he didn't stop.

"Isaiah," Ruthie interrupted gently, trying to get his attention. "You have a customer."

Isaiah turned around, saw the customer, but then turned

back to Ruthie, continuing his explanation. "Like I was saying, it's about maintaining balance. And finding that balance is key, you know? It's like, if I let one thing slip, everything else follows, and then I suffer. So, I must be strict with myself. But I'm sure your treats are amazing. Everyone says so."

Ruthie managed a smile, feeling slightly overwhelmed by his lengthy account.

Isaiah nodded decisively, seemingly unaware of his impatient customer waiting behind him. "Thanks for the basket. If you want to leave it, I'll have my customers try them and tell you their favorites."

Confused by his strange mannerisms, she placed the basket on the workbench and smiled at Jedediah. "I'm sorry for the wait," she said kindly. "He can be a bit… focused."

The man nodded, his eyes following Ruthie as she walked out. As she walked back to the bakery, Ruthie muttered to herself, "I've never met a man who didn't eat sweets. How could I ever imagine anything with someone who doesn't approve of them? It's like oil and vinegar, a combination that doesn't mix."

She shook her head, still unsure about Isaiah. Despite his strange habits and constant chattering, she couldn't deny that he fascinated her. Perhaps they could find common ground, even if it wasn't over sweets.

Back at the bakery, Ruthie resumed her work, but her thoughts kept drifting back to Isaiah. She wondered what other quirks he had and how they might impact any potential friendship. She was set on understanding him better, even if it meant stepping out of her comfort zone to figure him out.

***

Jedediah patiently waited for his turn at the buggy shop. He had a reputation in Willow Springs for running a small, struggling bulk food store on the outskirts of town. He was known for his envious nature, always comparing his failing business to the success of others in the community. His eyes darted around Isaiah's shop, taking in every detail.

"Sorry to keep you waiting," Isaiah finally addressed him, snapping out of his focused state.

"No problem," Jedediah replied, his words smooth, but his eyes calculating. "I was just admiring your shop. You've done a good job fixing it up."

"Thanks," Isaiah said, still a bit distracted. "What can I do for you today?"

Jedediah gestured to the buggy seat he had brought in with him. "I was hoping you could reupholster this for me. It's seen better days, and I hear you might be able to help me."

Isaiah examined the seat, nodding thoughtfully. "I can do that. Shouldn't take too long."

Understanding, Jedediah nodded, seemingly satisfied. "I tried to fix it myself, but I don't have the right tools for the job." Jedediah paused and looked around the shop. "What other plans do you have for this place?"

Isaiah looked up, surprised by the question. "Well, just trying to keep up with the work and maybe expand a bit. There's always something to fix or improve."

Jedediah's eyes narrowed slightly as he probed further. "Sounds like you're doing well here. Must be nice to have the funds to expand."

Isaiah shrugged, still focused on the buggy seat. "Just taking it one day at a time. Anything else you need?"

Jedediah shook his head, an envious smile playing on his lips. "No, that's all for now. Thanks, Isaiah. I'll be back to check on the seat."

***

Isaiah's thoughts lingered on Ruthie. He hadn't meant to disappoint her, but he needed to be up front. It was better to set the right expectations than risk misunderstanding later. Despite the awkwardness of their conversation, he wanted to know more about her. He admired her determination and strong will. But his mind was abruptly pulled back to reality when he heard someone clearing their throat behind him. He turned around, finally acknowledging a new customer. The man looked slightly annoyed but masked it with a polite smile.

"Can I help you?" Isaiah asked, his voice steady.

The man pushed a photo under Isaiah's nose. "Have you seen this man around?"

Isaiah barely glanced at the picture of a man about his age with a stern expression. Isaiah handed it back, shaking his head. "Just moved to the area. Everyone's a stranger to me. Haven't had time to notice anyone specific."

Isaiah studied the man for a moment, noting details someone else might miss. The man's clothes were clean, his shoes polished but not new, and his hair neatly trimmed. There was an air of urgency about him, and he seemed to be trying too hard to blend in. Something about him felt off, but Isaiah couldn't quite put his finger on it.

"Why did you move to Willow Springs?" the man asked abruptly, his tone probing.

Isaiah kept his eyes neutral, though he felt a surge of irritation. "Seemed like a good place to build my business."

The man tilted his head slightly, his eyes narrowing. "This business?"

Isaiah shook his head. "Yep, buggy shop."

The man nodded slowly as if considering Isaiah's words. "Alright. It was a long shot. Thanks."

"Of course," Isaiah replied politely, though inwardly, he was growing tired of the questioning. He had chosen this business precisely because he expected fewer interactions with *Englishers*, who often asked too many questions and pried into matters that were none of their business.

The man thanked him and left, but not before giving Isaiah one last lingering look. Isaiah returned to his work, but his mind kept drifting back to the photo... He knew exactly who it was, Evert Miller, his drifter cousin who had jumped the fence to the *Englisch* a long time ago.

The sound of the door opening interrupted his thoughts

again. Another customer had entered, and Isaiah quickly shifted his focus, greeting the Amish man with a friendly smile. But even as he worked, his mind continued to turn over the details of the day, filing away every small clue and observation until later, when he could make a note of them properly.

CHAPTER 4

The next morning, Ruthie was busy making lemon pie filling when the bell above the door jingled. She looked up to see Isaiah stepping into the bakery, carrying the basket she had given him the day before.

Isaiah greeted her with a small smile. "I wanted to return this to you."

Ruthie nodded. "Did you change your mind about trying some samples?"

Isaiah shook his head. "No, but I wanted to talk to you about something else. Yesterday, after you left, a man stopped in and showed me a photo of a man with dark curly hair, brown eyes, and a scar on his chin. He was asking if I'd seen him around."

Ruthie stopped stirring the thick filling and let out a small gasp. "That sounds like the man who came into the bakery asking questions about my ingredients." She shuddered and shook her head. "He seemed way too interested in the bakery, and he made me uncomfortable." Ruthie sighed as she processed the information. "So, we've both had encounters with strange men asking questions. What do you think it means?"

Isaiah sighed softly. "I'm not sure."

Ruthie felt a surge of determination. "We can't stand back and do nothing. This is affecting our businesses, my friends, and our community. We need to figure out what's going on, and as far as the police are concerned, it doesn't warrant their time."

Isaiah's head tilted as he nodded in thought, meeting her gaze. "I agree. We need to be careful who we talk to and how we answer strange questions."

Ruthie smiled, feeling a sense of camaraderie with him.

Isaiah returned the smile, appreciating Ruthie's boldness. "Sounds like a plan. I'll keep my eyes and ears open, and we can compare notes at the end of the day."

Isaiah looked up and down the street before he rounded the corner to head back to his shop. He didn't like the thought of people hanging around asking questions... especially about Evert. But more importantly, he didn't like his cousin, scaring Ruthie with his strange visit. That could only mean he was close to figuring out more clues. He certainly didn't need to bring too much attention to himself. He needed to keep his guard up, and

Isaiah needed to make sure Evert kept Ruthie out of his plans.

***

Later that evening, Ruthie and Isaiah met at the bakery after closing. The shop was quiet, the aroma of freshly baked goods still lingered in the air. They sat at a small table near the window, each with a cup of coffee in hand.

"I talked to a few customers today," Ruthie began, pulling out a notepad. "I've written down everything I know." She meticulously outlined her notes, detailing the strange man's behavior and the questions he asked.

Isaiah chuckled, reaching into his pocket and pulling out his own list. "Looks like we both have a knack for list-making," he said with a grin.

Ruthie smiled, feeling a bit more at ease. "Great minds think alike."

As Ruthie went over her notes, Isaiah listened intently, his knee bouncing and his fingers tugging at his shirt. Ruthie paused, watching his movements with curiosity. Isaiah seemed to notice and stopped, giving her an apologetic look.

"Sorry, old habits," he said sheepishly.

"It's alright," Ruthie replied. "Let's go over what we have." They compared notes, piecing together the information they had gathered. Just as they were deep in discussion, the door to the bakery opened, and Annie stepped inside.

"Ruthie, Isaiah," Annie greeted, looking slightly out of breath. "I found out something about the missing ledger."

Ruthie and Isaiah turned their attention to her, eager for any new information.

"My grandparents couldn't remember anything specific about the ledger. All they could remember was that one of the ledgers had a strange riddle written on the inside cover. I haven't had time to go through all the ledgers to see if I can locate the one they're talking about. If I can't find it, then we'll know it was the one stolen."

Ruthie tapped her thumb on the notebook on the table. "That's so strange. There was a short riddle etched on my recipe's box inside cover." She crossed her arms and leaned back in her chair. "I'm not sure I can remember exactly what it said. Something about pinwheels and shadows."

Annie pulled a note out of her pocket. "All my grandmother could remember was the riddle in the ledger had something to do with iron and flames."

"That's strange!" Isaiah ran a hand through his hair.

Annie nodded. "It's possible that the ledger might hold some clues. But I find it odd that both missing items may have contained riddles."

Ruthie looked thoughtful. "So, the ledger could be connected to the recipe box. And if that's the case, it might explain why someone is so interested in it now."

Isaiah leaned back, his mind racing. "We need to find that ledger or why someone would want it."

Ruthie nodded, feeling a renewed sense of purpose. "We're getting closer to understanding this. Let's keep digging and see where it leads us."

Annie added, "I'll spend some time looking through all the ledgers. There are over one hundred of them to go through. *Mamm* said there are boxes of them in the attic from the early 1900s."

As they continued to discuss their next steps, they compared notes and wondered what both the Quilt Market and the bakery had in common.

***

Isaiah walked to his buggy shop, enjoying the cool and crisp night air. The conversation with Ruthie and Annie had left his mind buzzing with questions and possibilities. As he unlocked the door to his small apartment at the back of the shop, he couldn't help but replay the evening's events in his head.

His apartment was modest, with just the essentials: a bed, a small kitchen area, and a small table cluttered with dirty dishes and notebooks containing all his notes and things he didn't want to forget to take care of. He poured himself a glass of water, and taking a sip, he leaned against the counter, his thoughts drifting back to Ruthie.

He was struck by how well they had worked together. Despite their initial awkward encounters, their collaboration tonight felt natural and effortless. He appreciated her determination and the way she meticulously took notes, mirroring his own methodical approach.

Isaiah moved to the table and began tinkering with a broken clock he had found at a thrift store. His hands worked automatically, but his mind was elsewhere. He thought about Ruthie's smile, her fiery spirit, and how she seemed genuinely interested in solving the mystery that had unsettled their community.

As he adjusted the gears of the clock, he couldn't help but think about their conversation. Ruthie had shown a vulnerability when she talked about the impact of the thefts on her business and her friends. It made him want to protect her, to ensure that nothing else disrupted her life.

Isaiah shook his head, trying to focus. This wasn't the time for distractions, but he couldn't deny his growing attraction toward Ruthie. She was unlike anyone he had ever met. He admired her resolve and the way she took charge, but there was also a softness in her that he found equally compelling.

He chuckled to himself, realizing how quickly his thoughts had turned from solving a mystery to thinking about Ruthie. He had never been good at reading social cues, but there was no mistaking the warmth he felt when he was around her. His heart raced a little faster, and he felt a strange but pleasant nervousness.

Isaiah set the clock down and walked over to the window. He looked out at the peaceful streets of Willow Springs. Meeting Ruthie and working together had made him feel like he was finally finding his place.

He had hoped to find a sense of belonging, and maybe even someone to share his life with. Could Ruthie be that person?

The thought both excited and terrified him.

Isaiah stared out the window as he remembered the way she had watched him fidget with his shirt and how she had kindly accepted his apology. She didn't seem put off by his quirks, which was a rare and comforting realization.

Working closely with Ruthie meant spending more time together, and he found himself looking forward to it. Maybe, in the midst of solving this mystery, they could also discover something more between them.

Isaiah shut his eyes, a small smile playing on his lips. He couldn't remember the last time he felt this hopeful.

***

The sun peeked through the curtains as Ruthie bustled around the kitchen, preparing breakfast. Her father, Amos, sat at the table, his face pale and drawn.

"*Datt*, you don't look well. Are you sure you're up for church today?"

Amos shook his head slowly, a cough racking his body. "*Nee*, I don't think I can make it today. You go on without me. I'll be fine here."

Ruthie frowned. "Are you sure? Maybe I should stay home and take care of you."

Amos waved his hand dismissively. "I'll be alright. Just need to rest. You go and keep the Lord's Day holy."

Giving a nod, Ruthie reluctantly, knowing how important it was to her father that she attend church. "Alright, *Datt*. But I'll be back right after the service to check on you."

***

Ruthie sat next to Annie in the row marked for unmarried girls, her mind drifting between the sermon and the recent events that had disrupted her life.

After the service, Ruthie noticed Hilda Hiltey, the owner of a bakery on the outskirts of town, standing by the kitchen door. Hilda was known for her donuts, but her business had seen a decline ever since Ruthie's bakery had gained popularity. Ruthie had always felt a slight tension between them, though they had never spoken much.

There was no way to enter the kitchen except to pass her, so Ruthie approached Hilda with a smile. "It's nice to see you," she greeted warmly.

Hilda glanced up, her face guarded and sharp. "*Jah,* it's always nice to gather with the community."

Tilting her head slightly, Ruthie asked, "How's your bakery doing?"

Hilda's eyes narrowed slightly, and she crossed her arms. "It's doing all right. Business isn't what it used to be, but we manage." With a sneer plastered on her lips, Hilda added, "I've come across some new recipes I want to try, and I'm eager to give my customers more options. Maybe even lure some of yours away."

Ruthie sensed the underlying bitterness in Hilda's mood.

Hilda's lips pressed into a thin line. "It must be nice having all those customers flocking to your bakery in town." Hilda squared her shoulders and whispered in a husky voice. "Isn't it about time you get married and give up this silly notion of owning a business?"

Ruthie felt irritated but maintained her composure. "We're all just trying to make a living. It's not about competition, and there are plenty of customers to go around."

With a firm nod, Hilda added curtly. "Indeed. But some of us have been doing this a lot longer and don't have the same… advantages."

"Even my sister's quilt shop could use more business. It seems like everyone prefers shopping in town rather than driving out to our cottage businesses."

Before Ruthie could respond, a group of women approached, interrupting their conversation. Hilda gave a polite nod and walked away, leaving Ruthie with a sense of unease.

Ruthie made her way to the kitchen to help with lunch preparations, feeling more of Hilda's resentment. Could her bitterness force her to do the unthinkable? The thought nagged at Ruthie, and she resolved to keep an eye on Hilda.

In the kitchen, Ruthie and Annie worked together, arranging moon pies on a tray. The air was filled with the delicious aroma of bean soup and friendly banter as the women busied themselves with lunch preparations.

"I had an interesting conversation with Hilda just now," Ruthie whispered to Annie as she filled another tray with the apple-filled moon pies.

Annie raised her eyebrow. "Oh? What did she have to say?"

Ruthie kept her voice low. "She's not happy about my bakery. She said I should be getting married and raising a family, not running a business that takes customers away from her home bakery. She even mentioned trying some new recipes to lure people away from my shop.”

Annie’s let out a small gasp. “*Ach*, she actually said that?”

Ruthie nodded. “*Jah*, and she made it clear she’s also upset about your quilt shop. They’re both sour about how our businesses are doing.”

Annie shook her head. “Hilda has always been a bit of a spinster. Never married, still living in the same farmhouse she was born in. I suppose she’s just set in her ways.”

Ruthie glanced around to make sure no one was listening. “Do you think she could be involved in the thefts? It seems strange that she’d be so bitter about our success.”

Annie considered this for a moment. “It’s possible. She might see it as a way to sabotage us and bring business back to her and Greta. But we can’t jump to conclusions. We need more information.”

With a reassuring nod, Ruthie felt a bit more relieved.

***

The men gathered around the long wooden table, talking and laughing as Ruthie and Annie brought out the steaming bowls of bean soup and baskets of bread. As Ruthie put down a bowl in front of Isaiah, she couldn't help but notice the way his eyes lingered on her, a hint of warmth in his eyes.

"Thank you, Ruthie," Isaiah said, his voice sincere.

Ruthie smiled, feeling a flutter in her chest. "You're welcome."

As the meal progressed, Ruthie and Annie continued to serve the men, their conversation from earlier still fresh in Ruthie's mind. She glanced over at Hilda, who stood at the far end of the room cutting slices of pie, her face stern and unapproachable.

When the meal was over, Ruthie started clearing the dishes and found a moment to speak to Isaiah privately.

"I had an interesting conversation with an older woman today who owns a bakery out by Highway 208," she said quietly.

Isaiah furrowed his brow. "Oh? What about?"

Ruthie explained Hilda's comments about her bakery and the quilt shop. "She seemed really bitter, and I can't help but wonder if she might somehow be involved in what's been going on... at least with my recipe box missing."

Isaiah frowned, considering this. "It's possible. But do you really think an old woman could pull off such things?"

"It's hard to believe someone would go that far, but we can't rule anything out."

Isaiah agreed. "I have an idea. She doesn't know me. Maybe I can stop in next week and keep my ears and eyes open to what she might be up to."

***

The rhythmic clopping of horse hooves echoed through the peaceful countryside as Hilda and her sister Greta made their way home from church. The sisters, both unmarried and set in their ways, wore an air of thinly veiled bitterness as they discussed the morning service and the younger generation's flourishing businesses.

"Did you see how Ruthie Mast acted?" Hilda sneered, gripping the reins tightly. "It's as if she doesn't have a care in the world, taking all our customers with her fancy bakery downtown."

Greta nodded, her eyes turning into slivers. "And Annie's family with their quilt shop. It's as if the whole community has forgotten about us out here. We've been doing this for decades, and now they think they can just come in and take over."

Hilda's lips curled into a smug smile. "Well, they'll have a surprise coming their way. I finally got my hands on some new secret recipes. It's like *Gott* finally answered our prayers, Greta. We can use those recipes to bring people back to our bakery."

"How did you manage that?"

Hilda chuckled softly. "Let's just say I have my ways. I've been trying for years to get my hands on some old recipes, and now we have them. We don't even have to feel bad about it. Anything we can do to drive customers back to our businesses is fair game."

Greta shifted uncomfortably in her seat, her expression softening. "I don't know, Hilda. Sometimes I feel bad that we're so bitter. This can't be good in the eyes of the Lord."

"Well, I'm tired of scrounging for Ruthie's scraps. We've worked hard for years, and now it's our turn to thrive. *Gott* helps those who help themselves, Greta. We need to do whatever it takes to bring people back to our bakery and your quilt shop."

Greta looked down at her hands, her guilt evident. "I suppose you're right. We need to help each other if we want to survive this decline. I'll add some samples of my quilts in your bakery, and you can add some of your baked items in my quilt shop. It's time we reminded everyone of the quality and tradition we offer."

"That's the spirit. We'll show them that the Hiltey sisters aren't to be underestimated."

As they approached their farmhouse, Hilda was confident that with the new recipes and their combined efforts, they could reclaim their lost customers and restore their businesses to their former glory.

As they pulled into their driveway, they saw a familiar figure waiting for them by the barn. Samuel Glick stood with his arms crossed, impatience etched on his face.

"Well, well, if it isn't our sneaky little businessman," Hilda muttered as they brought the buggy to a stop.

Samuel approached them, not wasting any time. "We need to discuss our plan further. I came to collect payment for the job I did for you."

Hilda climbed down from the buggy and gave Samuel a sharp look. "You'll get your payment, but not a minute before our new plans take shape."

"I did what you asked. Now it's time to settle up."

Hilda stood her ground, unflinching. "You got us what we needed, but we haven't seen the results yet. You'll be paid once we start seeing a return on our investment. Not before."

Samuel clenched his jaw, his frustration evident. "That's not how business works… especially mine. I expected to be paid when the goods were delivered."

Hilda crossed her arms, a steely glint in her eyes. "Then perhaps you should have considered that before agreeing to the job. You'll get paid when we see our plan worked. Not a minute sooner."

Greta, sensing the tension, stepped forward, her voice softer. "Hilda's right, Samuel. We're grateful for your help, but we need to make sure this works before we can pay you." Samuel turned to leave, pausing only for a moment.

"Two weeks… I'll give you two weeks, and I'll be back, expecting to be paid."

Hilda felt a surge of satisfaction as she watched him walk away. She wasn't about to let a young, snotty-nose boy like Samuel intimidate her. She had what she needed and would see to it that their businesses thrived once more.

Once Samuel was out of earshot, Greta sighed deeply, her conscience weighing on her. "Hilda, do you really think this is what *Gott* wants for us? It feels so wrong."

"We've worked hard for years and deserve to see the fruits

of our labor. We can't let Ruthie and her fancy bakery drive us out of business."

Greta looked down; her guilt evident. "I just hope we're not making a mistake. Being so hateful doesn't feel right."

Hilda placed a firm hand on her sister's shoulder. "It's just business. Sometimes, to survive you must do things that aren't pleasant. We'll make this work, and our customers will see we can adapt to their changing taste buds."

CHAPTER 5

As Ruthie made her way home from the Hostetler's, the afternoon sun filtered through the trees lining both sides of Spring Quarry Road. The soft scent of blooming lilacs and mowed grass filled the air, mingling with the distant sound of robins chirping. She was lost in thought, replaying her conversation with Hilda, when she heard footsteps approaching.

"Ruthie," Samuel called out as he came up to her. He had a smug smile on his face, which only made Ruthie more annoyed.

"Hello," she replied curtly, quickening her pace.
Samuel kept stride with her. "You're always in such a hurry. What's the rush?"

Ruthie sighed, a look of resignation on her face. "I have things to do, Samuel. And I prefer to walk alone."

Samuel chuckled, not taking the hint. "You're always so serious, Ruthie. I was hoping we could talk more. You know, get to know each other better."

Ruthie stopped and turned to face him. "I don't have time for idle chatter, Samuel. I have a business to run, and I'm trying to figure out who stole my family's recipe box. I didn't memorize some of those recipes, and it's a big loss for the bakery."

Samuel's smile faded, replaced by a look of irritation.

Ruthie's patience was wearing thin. "What do you want, Samuel?"

Before he could respond, a neighbor stopped his buggy beside them, looking distressed. His weathered skin and clothes that were too big for his small frame made him look aged beyond his years. His clothes were in need of repair, adding to his haggard appearance. He never stepped down from his buggy, clearly in a hurry to get back home.

"There's been a break-in at *Noah's Harness Shop*," he said, his voice tinged with urgency.

Ruthie's face went pale. "A break-in? What happened?" Jedediah Weaver, the neighbor, shook his head. "Someone broke the lock off the back door. Looks like they were looking for something. Only one thing was stolen, though—an old map that Noah had framed and hung behind the counter. They broke the glass and just took the map."

Ruthie glanced at Samuel, then back at Jedediah. "An old map? Why would anyone steal that?"

Jedediah shrugged, his eyes darting around nervously. "Who knows? But it's got everyone on edge. I just thought you should know." He tipped his hat and flicked the reins, his buggy moving off quickly as he headed back home.

Ruthie instantly felt the break-in had to be connected to the bakery and quilt shops. "We need to go check on Noah."

Samuel hesitated, clearly not eager to get involved. "I'm sure Noah can handle it. Besides, what's the point?"

Ruthie shot him a sharp look. "What else do you have to do, Samuel? Come on, let's go."

Samuel reluctantly agreed, and they hurried toward the harness shop. As they walked at a quick pace, Ruthie couldn't help but notice Samuel's lack of interest in the break-in. It struck her as odd, but she pushed the thought aside, focusing on helping Noah.

When they arrived at the harness shop, the scene was chaotic. Noah stood in the middle of the shop, surveying the damage with a look of frustration.

"Noah, are you alright?" Ruthie asked, rushing to his side.

Noah sighed heavily. "I'm fine. Just frustrated. They made such a mess for an old map. I don't understand it."

Ruthie looked around at the destruction, her mind was a chaotic storm. "What would anyone want with an old map?"

"It's just an old map of Willow Springs. I've had it for years. Can't imagine why anyone would want it."

Detective Powers stepped into the shop, a notepad in hand. "We're trying to piece that together, Ms. Mast. Seems odd to go through all this trouble for an old map."

Noah picked up the broken frame and pieced it back together, showing Ruthie the back. "It even had this note etched on the back of the frame."

"The key you hold, the map's path shows. Beneath the bench, treasures glow." Ruthie read the words aloud, her brow furrowed. "What does that mean?"

Detective Powers jotted down the note in his pad. "It's definitely cryptic. We'll have to look into it further. Noah, did you notice anything else missing or out of place?"

"No, just the map. The frame it was in was probably worth more than the map itself."

"Detective, do you think the break-ins are connected? The one at my bakery and now this?"

Detective Powers closed his notebook. "At this point, it's

hard to say. The items taken are so specific and seemingly unrelated. But we can't rule out the possibility."

Ruthie's mind raced with thoughts. "Detective, is there anything we can do to help?"

Detective Powers gave a small smile. "Just keep your eyes and ears open. Sometimes the smallest detail can be the key to solving a case. And if you think of anything, no matter how insignificant it might seem, let me know."

Samuel, who had been lingering near the door, finally spoke up. "Maybe it's not the map itself, but something about it that's important."

Ruthie turned to him, surprised by his insight. "You might be right, Samuel. We need to figure out what's so special about that map."

Noah nodded with a look of despair covering his face. "I just don't understand what value the old map had to anyone."
As they worked together to clean up the shop, Ruthie couldn't help but think that all the break-ins were connected… but how?

***

The next day, Ruthie explained the events to Isaiah when he

stopped in to pick up his standing order. Isaiah listened intently, but Ruthie noted a flicker of something in his eyes when she mentioned Samuel.

"So, Samuel was with you when you found out about the break-in?" Isaiah asked, trying to keep his tone casual.

With a determined nod, Ruthie continued. "*Jah*, he was. He didn't seem too eager to help at first, though."

Isaiah's mood darkened slightly. "I don't know much about Samuel, but he doesn't seem to be interested in anyone but himself."

Ruthie let out a sigh. "He's not my favorite person, but we needed all the help we could get."

Isaiah seemed off for the rest of the conversation, and Ruthie couldn't help but pry a little. "Is something bothering you?"

Isaiah shook his head, but Ruthie could tell he was holding something back.

Isaiah hesitated for a moment before blurting out, "Are you interested in Samuel?"

"What? No, of course not. Why would you think that?" Isaiah looked down and shuffled his feet, tugging at his shirt. "I don't know. I guess I just... I don't like the idea of you being around him."

Ruthie's heart softened. "Isaiah, I'm not interested in Samuel."

Silence filled the air for a few seconds before Isaiah added, "There must be something significant about the map."

Ruthie nodded. "I agree. Maybe it points to something valuable, or a hidden secret in Willow Springs."

Isaiah leaned forward; his appearance serious. "We need to find out more about that map and why it was important enough to steal, but where do we start?"

"I'm not sure. I know the library has a map room, perhaps they have all the old maps of Lawrence County."

Isaiah and Ruthie were still discussing the map when Samuel walked in. Ruthie noticed a sudden change in Isaiah's stance as soon as Samuel sauntered up to the counter. Isaiah quickly excused himself, telling Ruthie they would discuss it further later.

Samuel leaned casually against the counter.

"What can I do for you?" Ruthie asked, trying to keep her tone neutral.

Samuel looked around the bakery, his eyes lingering on the fresh pastries. "Just thought I'd stop by and see how you're doing after yesterday's events."

"It's been a busy morning, so I haven't had much of a chance to think about things too much."

Samuel responded with a nod, a thoughtful look on his face. "You know, it's strange how things started going haywire around here right after Isaiah showed up. Don't you think?"

Ruthie frowned. "What are you getting at, Samuel?"

Samuel shrugged. "Just something to think about. It's quite a coincidence. First, the recipe box, the ledger at the Quilt Market, and now the break-in at Noah's shop. Makes you wonder, doesn't it?"

Ruthie had her doubts but quickly pushed them aside. "Isaiah has been nothing but helpful since he arrived. I trust him."

Samuel raised an eyebrow. "Do you really? How well do you know him, Ruthie? People aren't always what they seem."

Ruthie's patience was wearing thin. "Thank you for your concern, Samuel, but I think I can judge for myself who I can depend on."

Samuel held up his hands in mock surrender. "Just trying to look out for you. I'd hate to see you get hurt."

As Samuel left, Ruthie couldn't shake the uneasy feeling his words had left behind. She tried to focus on her work, but doubts about Isaiah started to creep in. What did she really know about Isaiah King? And she couldn't help but remember he took off right after lunch, and she didn't see him again until that morning. Would he have had time to drive out to Noah's and get back before Noah returned home from church?

***

The Quilt Market was unusually quiet as Annie arranged the latest bolts of fabric. The soft rustle of the fabrics and the faint tick of the wall clock were the only sounds in the cozy shop. As she placed a particularly vibrant piece of cloth on the shelf, the bell above the door tinkled softly, signaling the arrival of a customer.

Annie looked up to see Eleanor Fischer stepping into the shop, her glare one of interest as she looked around the fabric store.

"Hello, Mrs. Fischer," Annie greeted warmly, though she felt a pang of wariness. "What can I help you with today?"

Eleanor offered a polite smile. "I wanted to find some information about an old Amish quilt pattern. Specifically, the pinwheel design.”

“The pinwheel design? That’s quite a specific request. Let me see what I can find.”

Annie walked over to the bookshelf that held the old ledgers, and she began scanning the spines for the familiar pinwheel design. Her heart skipped a beat when she realized that the ledger from 1980, the one with the pinwheel design, was the one that must have been stolen. They only had one ledger for each design, so it was easy to figure out that was the missing one.

“That’s strange,” Annie muttered, more to herself than to Eleanor.

Eleanor stepped closer. “What’s strange?”

Annie turned to her; concern etched on her face. “The ledger from 1980, which features the pinwheel design, must be the one that was taken a few days ago. We couldn’t know for sure which design was featured on the cover, but it makes sense now that I can’t find that book.”

Eleanor’s eyes lifted slightly, but she quickly composed herself.

“That’s odd. I’ve been doing some research about that design and figured you or your parents would be the ones to ask about it."

Annie had always been wary of Eleanor, knowing the *Englisch* historian had a reputation for stirring up trouble. "Why are you researching it?"

Eleanor hesitated for a moment before answering. "I'm working on a historical piece about folklore in small towns. This pattern is linked to an old tale from over thirty years ago."

Annie nodded slowly, still processing the information. "Well, I hope you find what you're looking for. But if you come across anything related to our missing ledger, please let us know."

"Of course, I'll be sure to keep you informed. I appreciate your help."

Annie wondered if she should have asked her more questions about the folklore, but she decided to go over it with Ruthie first as soon as she closed for the day. She felt it was strange that Eleanor was researching a story that involved the pinwheel design at that very moment.

***

Eleanor Fischer walked away from the Quilt Market, a

satisfied smile tugging at the corners of her mouth. She had spent the last fifteen years following clues, inching closer and closer to the treasure that had eluded so many. She wasn't about to give up now, not when she was so close.

"They have no idea," she thought, her fingers brushing the edges of the notebook tucked safely in her coat pocket.

Eleanor knew more about the missing ledger than she had let on. It had taken years of careful research and countless dead ends, but she had finally pieced together enough of the puzzle to see the bigger picture. The pinwheel design was the key, a symbol that connected everything. But she was still missing a few clues… especially the map and its role.

"I need to keep them distracted," she mused, her eyes tightened as she walked. "If they start digging too deep, they might stumble onto something I don't want them to find. Not yet."

Eleanor's thoughts drifted back to the small town, the quaint shops, and the unsuspecting residents. She had grown fond of Willow Springs in her own way, but business was business. And finding the treasure meant everything to her—the culmination of years of work and the promise of a new beginning.

As she walked through the quiet streets, she replayed the information she had gathered in her mind. She needed to figure out how they all fit together.

"They'll never suspect me," she thought, a confident smile spreading across her face. "By the time they realize what's really going on, I'll be long gone—with the treasure."

Eleanor quickened her pace, feeling the thrill of the hunt coursing through her veins. She had to stay one step ahead, had to keep her wits about her. The townspeople of Willow Springs were just pieces to be played, and she intended to use them all to her advantage.

As she rounded the corner, she spotted the county records building. She needed to find more information about her family's land.

The records building was noiseless, the scent of old paper and ink filling the air. Eleanor made her way to the archives section, pulling out several dusty volumes and settling into a corner to read. Hours passed as she pored over old documents and maps, her notebook filling with scribbled notes and observations.

Finally, as the building was about to close, she stumbled upon a passage that caught her attention. Her heart raced as she realized she was on the right track.

Eleanor closed the book with a satisfied smile and stood up, her mind buzzing with new possibilities. She was getting closer, and she knew it. All she needed was a little more time and a few more pieces of the puzzle.

The treasure was within her grasp, and she wouldn't let anything—or anyone—stand in her way. She glanced back at the quiet town, a place that had become the key to her ultimate success. "They'll never know what hit them," she thought, her smile turning into a smirk.

***

Ruthie was busy preparing for the next day when Annie rushed in.

"I have news," Annie exclaimed, barely catching her breath.

Ruthie looked up from her work. "What is it?"

Annie quickly explained Eleanor Fischer's visit and her interest in the pinwheel design. "She mentioned that she was doing some research on the pinwheel design, and it had something to do with old folklore from over thirty years ago. Don't you find that odd?"

"A pinwheel design? And that's the ledger that's missing? This can't just be a coincidence. There's definitely something more to this."

Annie acknowledged with a nod. "We need to find out what was in that ledger. It might hold the key to solving its disappearance. But I also think we need to talk to Isaiah. He's been helpful."

Ruthie hesitated, her mind flashing back to Samuel's words of doubt. "I don't know, Annie. You can't believe a word Samuel says, but he has got me thinking about just how much I know about Isaiah. What if he's involved somehow?"

Annie looked at her friend, surprised. "Ruthie, you're being silly. Isaiah has been nothing but kind and helpful."

Ruthie was conflicted but knew Annie was right. "Alright. Let's talk to Isaiah. But we also need to ask Noah about the map and if it had any clues that would match it to the pinwheel design."

Annie smiled, relieved. "Good. Let's go see Isaiah and then head to Noah's."

***

Isaiah stood at his workbench meticulously going over his to-do list, making sure he didn't forget anything when Ruthie and Annie burst into the shop.

Isaiah looked up, surprise flickering across his face.

Annie quickly explained all they'd discovered about Eleanor Fischer's visit and her interest in the pinwheel design. "She mentioned that the pinwheel design was a clue in some old story. We find that strange."

Isaiah took a seat at his bench and thought long and hard for a few moments. "It can't be a coincidence. The recipe box, the missing ledger, and the pinwheel design must be connected."

Ruthie watched his reaction closely, remembering Samuel's words.

Isaiah continued, oblivious to Ruthie's inner turmoil. "We need to find out more about the map that was stolen from Noah's shop. It might have clues that connect everything."

Annie stepped in, trying to ease the tension she saw etched across Ruthie's forehead. "We need to go talk to Noah and see if the map has any clues."

***

Ruthie, Annie, and Isaiah walked into Noah's shop, determined to find more information. The small harness shop was cluttered with tools and leather straps, remnants of the recent break-in still evident. Noah looked up from the mess, his look wary but curious.

"Noah, we need to ask you about your map," Ruthie said, her voice steady.

Noah looked up from the bridle he was working on and nodded. "What about it?"

Annie explained their findings about the pinwheel design and its connection to the missing ledger. "We think there's a connection between Ruthie's stolen recipe box, our quilt ledger, and your missing map. Do you remember any details about the map?"

Noah thought for a moment, then nodded. "The map had a lot of old markings and notes on it. My *datt* kept it around for some reason, but I never paid much attention to it.

There were a few symbols and designs on it, but I can't remember all the details."

As Noah spoke, Annie picked up a scrap piece of paper and began to hand-sketch the pinwheel design. She held it up for Noah to see. "Does this look familiar?"

Noah squinted at the drawing. "*Jah*, that design was definitely on the map. It was right in the center, with other smaller ones around it."

Isaiah leaned in, looking at the sketch. "What were the other symbols?"

Noah shrugged. "Guess I didn't pay too much attention, but I think smaller versions of the pinwheel design. All I know is it was like no other map I'd ever seen of the area."

"We need to find out more about that map. We think it's the key to solving these thefts," Ruthie inserted.

Noah's expression grew more serious. "You know, I did see something strange on Saturday. There was a man hanging around the shop. I hadn't seen him before, and he looked out of place. I was so busy that he eventually left before I could help him."

"Can you describe him?" Ruthie asked.

Noah's head bobbed as he thought back. "He was tall, with dark curly hair and a scar on his chin. Seemed like he was waiting for something or someone."

Isaiah's face turned pale, and he began to fidget, his knee bouncing uncontrollably as he sat on the stool at the workbench. Ruthie detected his sudden change in demeanor, and suspicion flickered in her mind.

"That description matches the man who came into my bakery asking questions." Ruthie's gaze sharpened as she glanced at Isaiah.

Isaiah forced a smile, trying to hide his discomfort. "It's probably just a coincidence."

Ruthie felt a knot of doubt tighten in her chest. Was Samuel right about Isaiah? She couldn't afford to ignore her instincts, especially with so much at stake.

As they left Noah's shop, Ruthie felt conflicted. There were still so many unanswered questions. She glanced at Isaiah, hoping he was the ally she needed in these increasingly suspicious events. Yet, the lingering doubt Samuel had planted in her mind refused to go away.

Isaiah's jittery behavior, combined with the description of the man who had been hanging around the harness shop, only deepened her uncertainty. She needed to figure out who she could truly trust. The mystery of the map and its connection to the pinwheel design on the ledger and her recipe box was crucial, but so was understanding the motives of those around her.

***

Later that evening, Isaiah sat at the table in his small apartment, deep in thought, as he replayed the clues over in his head. Everything was quiet, the only sounds being his ticking clock and the distant chirping of peepers outside.

He had a habit of doodling to keep his hands busy, and today was no different. He picked up a pencil and absentmindedly started to sketch on a blank sheet of paper.

His mind raced with the events of the past few days. The mysterious recipe box, the missing ledger, and the now stolen map. He could feel the pieces of the puzzle slowly coming together, but something was still missing. He needed a breakthrough, a clue that would show him he was on the right path.

As he doodled, his pencil traced over the paper, creating random shapes and lines. Suddenly, he felt the texture change beneath his pencil, as if there were indentations on the paper.

Curious, he began to shade over the area lightly. Gradually, a series of words started to appear, coming through his pencil marks like a hidden message being revealed.

Isaiah's heart raced as he continued shading, the words

becoming clearer and more defined: *Seek the harness that guides the way. Where secrets lie and history stays.*

He stared at the message; his brain was buzzing with ideas. This was it—the message pointed directly to *Noah's Harness Shop*. The old blacksmith shop, now his buggy shop, had been hiding this clue all along.

This was a significant breakthrough, but it also meant he was getting closer to something important, something that others were also desperate to find.

Isaiah carefully folded the sheet of paper and placed it in his pocket. He took a deliberate breath and looked around the shop, trying to steady his nerves. He couldn't afford to let his guard down now. He was getting closer to the truth, and he had to be ready for whatever came next.

Isaiah studied the table. It looked as if it had been there since the shop was first constructed. He traced his fingers over the worn surface, his mind drifting back to a conversation with his father.

His *datt* had handed him the deed to the old building that had been in his family for over thirty years with a hopeful look in his eye. "If anyone can figure out the old family legend, it'd be you," he had said with a laugh, sending Isaiah on his way.

The memory was as clear as day, and now he wondered if this table held the clue his father had teased him about.

Was this the clue his father had mentioned? Isaiah's heart pounded as he considered the possibility. It made sense that his *datt* would leave him with a puzzle to solve, something to test his wit and determination. He had always enjoyed solving problems, and this felt like the ultimate challenge.

The one who came upon it first would be the rightful owner. He never trusted his cousin, and he wasn't about to let him get the upper hand this time either. No matter how hard he tried to have a soft spot for the man, Evert was nothing but trouble, and he was having a hard time trusting his change of character.

It was good that he jumped the fence to become *Englisch* years earlier; he brought problems everywhere he went. Blood relatives or not, Isaiah didn't want him anywhere near his new friends or Willow Springs.

The sooner he solved the mystery, the better for everyone around. He had to keep things a secret from Ruthie for a while longer. He didn't dare put her or Annie in harm's way.

The connection between the old family legend and the current mystery was too strong to ignore. He just hoped they could unravel the secrets hidden within Willow Springs before it was too late.

He walked toward the door to lock up and saw a small piece of paper had been slipped under it. Frowning, he bent down and picked it up, unfolding it carefully. His eyes scanned the handwritten note, and his heart skipped a beat.

Remember, blood runs thicker than water. The past always catches up with us, cousin. Be prepared when it does.

Isaiah's mind raced as he read the note. He went to the door and glanced up and down the alley. With a determined look, he grabbed a lighter from his workbench and set the note aflame, watching as the paper curled and blackened before turning to ash.

As the last embers died out, Isaiah's thoughts returned to the events of the day. The visit to Noah's shop, the conversations with Ruthie and Annie—it all seemed connected. The note only added more urgency to the situation.

Isaiah moved back to his tiny apartment at the back of his shop. The small space was cluttered with papers, maps, and notes. He went back over his notes and tried to make sense of the clues. And now, with his discovery pointing to the harness shop, he was sure he was getting closer.

His thoughts drifted to Ruthie, to the way she had looked at him with suspicion. He couldn't blame her; after all, he was protecting secrets. But it was for a good reason, and he hoped she would understand once he was free to explain.

CHAPTER 6

The dim glow of the kerosene lamp lit the small, cluttered kitchen as Hilda stood over the counter, carefully measuring out ingredients. Her plump form hovered over the table, her graying hair pulled back into a tight bun, and her aged features set in a determined scowl. Her sister, Greta, sat at the table, her thin, wiry frame contrasting sharply with Hilda's. Greta's face twisted in distaste as she sampled yet another batch of lemon pie filling.

"Ugh, Hilda, this isn't right either," Greta said, pushing the bowl away. "I don't think you've got the lemon oil measurement correct. Something's off."

Hilda scowled. "It's hard to tell. The exact measurement is faded on this old recipe card. But I know I'm close."

Greta leaned back in her chair. "Maybe it's because we're going about this all wrong. Maybe we're not meant to get it right because of the way you got these recipes."

"Nonsense. This is our way to reclaim our place in this community, and these recipes are our way to do that."

Greta took another hesitant bite, wincing at the overly tart flavor. "Hilda, you've been at this all day. It's late, and you're exhausted. Maybe it's time to call it a night."

Hilda shook her head, staring intently at the faded recipe card. "I'm not giving up. Just go to bed. I'll figure it out one way or another."

With a sigh of resignation, Greta stood up and headed towards the stairs. "Fine, but don't stay up too late. We have a busy day tomorrow with getting ready for the quilt frolic."

Greta disappeared upstairs, and Hilda continued to study the recipe card, holding it closer to the lamp. The kitchen was saturated with the sweet and tangy scent of lemon, but the exact flavor eluded her. She was determined to make it perfect... even better than her competitor.

The late-night sounds of the spring evening drifted through the open screen door, but they did little to calm Hilda's mood. She was tired and frustrated, and the old recipe card was worn and faded, the handwriting barely legible in places. She squinted at the measurements, trying to decipher the missing details.

The kitchen clock ticked loudly in the quiet night, marking the passage of time. Hilda's mind raced as she mixed yet another batch, expecting this one to be the key to perfecting the recipe.

Hilda's thoughts wandered as she worked, thinking back to their childhood in the old farmhouse. They had always been taught to work hard and persevere, despite the obstacles. This was just another challenge, another obstacle to overcome. She would find the right balance, no matter how long it took.

Driven by desperation, Hilda continued to test and tweak the recipe as the night wore on. With a final sigh, Hilda put down her mixing spoon and stared at the latest batch. She dipped a spoon into the filling and tasted it, her brow furrowing. It still wasn't right, but she was getting closer. She knew it.

Exhausted but unwilling to give up, she finally decided to call it a night. She turned off the lamp and headed to bed, her mind still racing with thoughts of recipes and measurements. As she lay in bed, a new thought crept into her mind.

"I need to get my hands on some of Ruthie's fry pies," she muttered to herself. "I need to know exactly what she's doing to make them so perfect."

Hilda pondered who she could convince to make a purchase

for her. The solution came quickly—Samuel Glick. He'd proven himself useful before, and she knew he could be discreet.

"I'll send word for Samuel to stop by tomorrow," she decided. "He'll get us those fry pies."

With that plan in mind, Hilda finally allowed herself to drift off to sleep.

***

The Quilt Market buzzed with the soft hum of conversation and the gentle rustle of fabric as a group of women gathered to work on a quilt for the upcoming benefit auction. The quilt rack stood at the center of the room, the vibrant quilt top stretched out and ready for their careful stitches.

Ruthie closed the bakery at noon and made her way next door. As she entered, she was greeted by the familiar faces of Annie, Lydia, and Martha, Annie's mother. Several other women from the community sat around the quilt rack including Greta and Hilda. The air was full of lighthearted chatter.

"Ruthie!" Annie called out, waving her over.

Ruthie smiled and took a seat next to Annie, picking up her

needle and thread. The women were already deep in conversation, their voices a soothing background as they worked on the quilt.

"Have you heard any more about the thefts?" Lydia asked, her brow furrowed as she threaded her needle.

Ruthie shook her head, her hands deftly stitching a tiny, precise pattern. "Not much. It's troubling, though. Someone is targeting our businesses, and we can't figure out why."

Greta, her thin frame hunched over her work, nodded in agreement. "It's unsettling. Whoever it is, they seem to know exactly what they're looking for."

Hilda, her bosom almost reaching the table, inserted with a hint of bitterness, "We don't know if it's one of our own or an outsider trying to cause trouble. Either way, it's causing a lot of worry."

Annie's needle paused for a moment as she considered the recent events. "Do you think it could be someone from outside the community? Someone who knows our routines and targets us when we're most vulnerable?"

Ruthie looked thoughtful. "It's possible. But how would they know about the specific items they're taking? They don't seem valuable to an outsider."

With a weary sigh, Lydia said. "It's like they're looking for something specific, something hidden in plain sight. But what could it be?"

Greta's eyes flickered with a hint of unease. "It makes me wonder if it's someone who knows more about our history than we realize. Someone with a personal vendetta or a deep-seated grudge."

Hilda's face turned sour, a fixed hard stare as she glanced at Ruthie. "Or maybe it's someone who's offended a customer. We all know how Ruthie can be with people."

Ruthie bristled at the insinuation. "Hilda, that's not fair. I treat my customers with respect, and I haven't done anything to drive them away. Besides, it's not just my bakery that's been targeted. The quilt shop and Noah's harness shop were hit too."

Annie nodded in agreement. "Ruthie's right. This doesn't seem to be about one person's behavior. It's bigger than that."

Hilda's lips pressed into a thin line. "Maybe. But it's suspicious that these things started happening right after that new fellow from Willow Brook showed up. Nobody seems to know much about Isaiah King, do we?"

All the women shook their heads in unison until Martha spoke up. "I heard his family owned the old blacksmith shop, and they don't live around these parts anymore." Martha paused to measure out more thread before she continued, "I remember my folks talking about some old tale about a hidden treasure that put a big wedge in their family. As far as I know, some of them picked up and moved to Mercer County. Just up and left everything they owned behind."

The tension around the quilt frame grew obvious as the women exchanged glances. Ruthie felt a pang of doubt but quickly pushed it aside. "Isaiah was the one who helped the bank guard during the robbery. If he had something to do with these thefts, why would he go out of his way to help?"

Lydia sighed. "We need to be careful about pointing fingers. We don't have all the facts yet. But it's true that the timing of Isaiah's arrival is curious."

The women continued to stitch in silence for a moment, each lost in their own thoughts. Finally, Lydia spoke up. "The church leaders are setting up a meeting to discuss this. They want to bring an end to the fear that's fallen on our community. We need to support each other and stay vigilant and not be so quick to jump to our own conclusions."

The soft murmur of agreement spread through the group, and the tension began to ease. As they resumed their work,

Ruthie couldn't help but feel a renewed sense of reservation about Isaiah.

Martha, Annie's mother, who had been quietly stitching, cleared her throat. "You know, this isn't the first time Willow Springs has faced unexplained thefts and disappearances."

Ruthie looked up, intrigued. "What do you mean?"

Martha's needle paused mid-stitch as she recalled the past. "Years ago, when I was a young woman, there was a series of strange incidents. Small things would go missing—tools, family heirlooms, even some old books. And there were a few disappearances that no one could explain. It caused quite a stir in the community."

Lydia leaned in; her interest piqued. "Disappearances? Who went missing?"

Martha continued. "Two young men. They were both in their twenties and gone one day without a trace. Their families were devastated. People whispered about it for years, but no one ever found out what happened to them. Some thought they'd run away, but others believed something more sinister was at play."

Hilda snorted. "Probably just boys being foolish. Nothing to do with what's happening now."

Ruthie felt a shiver run down her spine. "But what if it is connected, Hilda? What if there's something we're not seeing?"

Greta, who had been unusually silent, spoke up. "It's possible. Sometimes, the past has a way of coming back to haunt us."

The room fell silent as the women absorbed Martha's story.

As the afternoon moved on, Hilda suggested a break. "Why don't we take a break and have a snack? Ruthie, maybe you could bring over some snacks from the bakery?"

Ruthie nodded in comprehension. "I can do that. I'll be right back."

She headed to the bakery and returned with a tray of assorted pastries, but not the coveted fry pies. Hilda's face fell when she saw the selection, and she wasn't shy about voicing her disappointment to Greta in hushed tones.

"Of course, she doesn't bring the fry pies," Hilda muttered. "She knows those are what everyone loves the most."

Greta, ever the voice of reason, tried to soothe her *schwester*. "Hilda, it's just a snack. Let it go."

Hilda huffed as she heavily sat her bottom back into her chair. "It's typical of her, though. Always keeping the best for her customers and leaving us with the leftovers."

Ruthie caught snippets of their conversation but chose to ignore it, focusing instead on distributing the pastries and making sure everyone was served. The tension around the quilt frame remained, the unspoken accusations hanging in the air like a dark cloud.

***

Later that evening, Hilda and Greta returned to their farmhouse, the conversation at the Quilt Market still fresh in their minds. Hilda's frustration with Ruthie had only grown.

"We need to get these lemon fry pies right, Greta," Hilda muttered, measuring out the ingredients with precision. "If we can't make them as good as Ruthie's, we're doomed."

Greta, her thin frame perched on a stool, tasted a spoonful of the lemon filling and made a face. "It's too tart."

Hilda slammed the spoon down, frustration boiling over. "I know it's not right! I can't get it perfect."

Greta sighed, her conscience weighing heavily on her. "Maybe this is a sign, Hilda."

Hilda shot her sister a sharp look. "Don't start with that again."

Greta shook her head, her frail hands wringing nervously. "But it's deceitful."

As the evening wore on, Hilda continued to experiment with the lemon filling, each failed attempt adding to her frustration. The sounds of the spring evening drifted in through the open screen door, but even the peaceful ambience couldn't calm her mood.

Finally, Greta gave up and headed to bed, disgusted by her sister's stubbornness. "I can't do this anymore, Hilda. Good night."

Hilda barely acknowledged her, her mind consumed by the task at hand. She stared at the faded measurement on the recipe card, willing it to reveal its secret.

***

Ruthie sat at the kitchen table, what was left of the day dipping below the horizon through the windows of her family's farmhouse. The familiar creak of the front door announced her father's arrival. Amos Mast, a sturdy man with graying hair and a kind face, entered the kitchen, stopping to wash his hands at the sink. He smelled of pine and diesel fumes, evidence of a long day spent at the lumber mill.

Ruthie set dinner on the table before him. As the only daughter left at home, she spent most of her evenings away from the bakery caring for her elderly father.

"Evening, *Datt*," she greeted, setting aside her teacup.

"How was your day?" he asked. "You look like you have something weighing on your shoulders this evening."

Ruthie hesitated for a moment before speaking. "I was hoping you might know something about something that I heard today."

"What kind of gossip did you women sputter up today?"

Ruthie giggled at his remark and asked, "Do you remember anything about a hidden treasure? One of the women at the quilt frolic mentioned it, and I was hoping you remember something about it."

Amos's eyes blinked with recognition. "Ah, that old story again," he remarked with an edge of irritation. "There was talk of a hidden treasure. It was said that it started as a game. Someone left clues all over town for someone to find. But what began as a game turned serious when some believed there was real treasure to be found. Caused quite a stir for some time."

Ruthie leaned in, eager for more details. "What kind of clues were they?"

Her father shrugged; his gaze distant as he tried to recall. "There were all sorts. Symbols, riddles, and maps. Folks thought it was just a story, but some took it seriously. There were rumors that the treasure was valuable, but no one ever found it as far as I know."

Ruthie's heart raced with excitement. "Do you think the recipe box with the pinwheel design could be one of those clues?"

Amos shifted uncomfortably in his chair as he gathered his words. "It's possible. That box just showed up. Got it as a wedding present, but I never figured out who it was from."

Ruthie felt a longing as she thought about her late mother. "I wish *Mamm* or *Grossmommi* were still around. They could have told me more about the recipes." Ruthie balanced her chin in the palm of her hand and sighed. "I'm afraid I relied on those recipe cards too much and have very few of them memorized."

She waited for a few seconds until her father cut his meatloaf with the back of his fork. "Do you know if there was anything special about the quilt design on the lid?"

Her father shook his head slowly. "I can't say for certain. Your mother always cherished that box, but she never mentioned anything about the design having special meaning. It's just one of those things that's always been."

"Do you think there's any way we could be related to the Kings?"

Amos chuckled softly. "In a small community like ours, everyone's related by marriage somewhere along the way. It's hard not to see one family merging into another over time. It wouldn't surprise me if there's a connection somewhere in our family tree."

Ruthie nodded. "Thanks, *Datt*. This helps a little."

Her father took a few seconds to wipe his mouth before adding, "Sometimes, digging up the past can bring more trouble than answers. And often, the past needs to stay right where it's at… in the past."

***

Evert sat hunched over the small desk in his dimly lit motel room, staring intently at his phone screen. The map of Willow Springs was displayed in a series of photographs he had taken, capturing every intricate marking and faded annotation. The map's key legend pointed to multiple locations scattered across the town, each spot marked with a small pinwheel design, adding to his growing frustration.

He rubbed his temples, trying to make sense of the chaotic pattern. "There's no rhyme or reason to these locations," he muttered. "The Mercantile, the old Methodist Church, the park in the center of town, the book shop, the library, the bakery, the old mill, the covered bridge, and a half dozen more were all marked with the same pinwheel symbol. It's maddening."

Evert picked up a pencil and began making a detailed list of all the marked locations; as he wrote them down, the list grew longer, and his frustration deepened. It would take him weeks, if not longer, to thoroughly investigate each site. The thought of the time it would consume left him feeling bitter and desperate.

He glanced at the phone screen again, trying to discern any hidden patterns or clues. Nothing made sense, and the randomness of the pinwheel markings was infuriating. He slammed his fist on the desk, causing his phone to fall to the floor. "Why couldn't they have made this simpler?" he growled.

Leaning back in his chair, he stared at the ceiling. He felt the pressure mounting, aware that others were tracking his every move. The fear of being caught was always at the back of his mind, but the desire for the hidden treasure pushed him forward.

He picked up the phone, examining the photos under the dim light. "I have to find it. I have to," he whispered to himself, determination mingling with his growing anxiety. The treasure was the key to everything. It could change his life, pull him out of hiding, and finally put an end to his restless wandering.

Evert stuffed the list into his coat pocket, slipped on his worn baseball cap, pulled it low over his eyes, and stepped out into the night. The cool air packed his lungs as he wandered down the quiet streets, following the clues to his first location. The treasure was out there, and he was determined to find it, no matter the cost. But he had to be cautious, for he wasn't the only one seeking it. And he couldn't afford to let anyone stand in his way.

CHAPTER 7

Ruthie was taking hot cinnamon rolls off their trays just as the bell above the door jingled.

Samuel stepped inside and glanced around the bakery, his gaze lingering on the assortment of pastries. "I'm here to buy one of everything you have in your bakery case."

Ruthie raised an eyebrow. "One of everything? That's quite a lot."

Samuel chuckled, attempting to appear casual. "I'm just in the mood to sample all your delicious treats. And, you know, I still want to build you another recipe box."

"You mentioned that before. Why are you so interested in my recipe box?"

Samuel leaned on the counter; his tone smooth. "I just think it's a shame that such a personal item was stolen. I want to make it up to you."

"And you don't have anything better to do," she asked as

she began packing up the various pastries.

"*Ack*, I have lots to do. But this is something I want to do." Ruthie looked at him suspiciously. "Since when do you think of anyone but yourself, and why am I so lucky?"

Samuel replied with a throaty chuckle. "If it helps me get what I want, I'll do almost anything; you should know that about me by now."

A burst of wind seeped into the shop as two men entered, stopping short of the counter, pretending to be engrossed in their conversation. Ruthie recognized them immediately as the two men she saw on the street shortly after someone stole her recipe box.

Trying to keep her composure, Ruthie handed Samuel the box jammed with pastries. "Here you go, enjoy."

As Samuel turned to leave, the two men approached the counter, and Samuel stopped short of the door. One of them, tall and lanky with a thin mustache, spoke first. "Good morning, ma'am. We're from the local newspaper, following up on a story about the recent thefts. Mind if we ask you a few questions?"

Ruthie's heart skipped a beat, but she kept her response neutral. "I'm sorry, but I know the local reporter, Jonas Butler, and you're not him. You should speak to Detective Powers at the Willow Springs Police Department."

The men exchanged a glance, and the other one, shorter with a shaved head, stepped forward. "We're just trying to gather some information, ma'am. The community needs to know what's going on."

Ruthie felt a chill run down her spine, but she remained firm. "I prefer not to answer any questions. Please take your inquiries to the police."

Samuel, sensing her discomfort, stepped closer to Ruthie. "Is there a problem here?"

The taller man shrugged. "No problem. We'll be on our way."

They both turned and left the bakery, casting lingering glances back at Ruthie and Samuel. Once they were gone, Ruthie let out a sigh of relief.

"Thank you for sticking around."

Samuel nodded. "They didn't seem like reporters to me."

Ruthie managed a small smile. "Me neither."

As Samuel turned to leave, he paused. "By the way, did you know Isaiah's family has connections to Willow Springs? I heard a rumor that they used to live here. Do you know anything about that?"

Ruthie looked up from wiping the counter. "*Nee*. Are you sure?"

Samuel responded with a nod. "That's what I heard. It makes me wonder why he's here, right?"

Ruthie felt a new seed of doubt take root in her mind once again. She had trusted Isaiah, but now she couldn't help but question his motives. "I'll look into it. Thanks for letting me know."

Samuel gave her a nod and left the bakery, leaving Ruthie to ponder his words.

***

Isaiah walked up to the bakery; his eyes were immediately drawn to the scene inside. Through the window, he saw Ruthie and Samuel in deep conversation. Samuel's sly smile was evident, and it made Isaiah's stomach churn. He could tell Samuel had ulterior motives, which bothered him more than he cared to admit.

Not wanting to interrupt or overhear anything, Isaiah decided to wait across the street on a park bench. He had things to discuss with Ruthie, and he wanted to avoid Samuel and the other two customers in the shop overhearing their conversation.

As he sat down, his fingers absently brushed against an etching on the wooden bench. Intrigued, he knelt to read the message carved into the bench seat: *"Where the pinwheel turns and shadows meet, go to the spot where secrets greet."*

Isaiah's mind raced. The message reminded him of the one he found etched on the table at the buggy shop: *"Seek the harness that guides the way, where secrets lie, and history stays."* Could these be connected? He quickly wrote down both messages in his notebook, making sure not to miss any details.

Lost in thought, he didn't notice time passing until he looked up and saw the two men leaving the bakery with Samuel not far behind. What struck him as odd was how they all disappeared into the alley between the Book Cellar and The Restaurant on the Corner. Something about them all heading in the same direction bothered him.

Isaiah crossed the street and entered the bakery, the bell above the door tinkling softly. He glanced around the empty shop, ensuring they were alone. "I need to talk to you, Ruthie. There's something I need to show you."

Ruthie nodded, sensing the urgency in his voice. "Let's sit

down," she suggested, leading him to a small table in the corner of the bakery.

Isaiah pulled out his notebook as they sat and showed her the messages he had copied. "I found this etched into a bench across the street," he explained, pointing to the first message. "And this one was etched into a table at the buggy shop."

Ruthie examined the notes, her brow furrowing. "*'Where the pinwheel turns and shadows meet, go to the spot where secrets greet'*," she read aloud. And *'Seek the harness that guides the way, where secrets lie, and history stays.'* This is getting more complicated."

"What did Samuel want?" Isaiah blurted out abruptly. "Pastries. I guess he was hungry. He bought one of everything I had in the case."

"You don't find that strange?"

"*Nee*, no stranger than you not wanting to taste even one bite."

They sat quietly for a moment before Ruthie couldn't stand it a minute longer and spilled what was on her mind. "Is there something you're not telling me? Samuel mentioned you might have family ties to Willow Springs."

Isaiah instantly started to bounce his knee and pull his

collar. "I do have family ties here. But those ties go way back before my time."

Ruthie hesitated, unsure whether to press the issue further. She decided to wait and listen, eager to gather more information before confronting him further. "So, what do you make of these clues?"

"Not sure… but they must lead to or mean something. Have you ever figured out the inscription in your mother's recipe box?"

Ruthie shook her head. "*Nee*. But I have an idea where I might be able to find out. My *mamm* loved to keep diaries, and there were boxes of them in the attic. My mother's things are very precious to my father, and he never wanted us girls to mess with them. I'm going to try to find some time to look through them."

Isaiah continued to fidget in his chair, making Ruthie wonder why he was suddenly acting so nervous. He was agitated more than normal, and his constant movement grated on Ruthie's last nerve, especially now that she was certain he wasn't telling her everything about his ties to Willow Springs.

As they worked on deciphering the clues, Ruthie noticed Isaiah's knee bouncing up and down, a sign of his restlessness.

"Do you always have to be moving?" she snapped.

A flash of embarrassment washed over Isaiah's face, and he purposely stopped his knee from shaking.

Suddenly, a lifetime of anxiousness about his disability covered him like the weighted blanket his mother used to try to get him to sleep under. The pain of being different stabbed him like a knife from the one person he thought could overlook his quirky personality. He immediately stood. "I've got to go."

Isaiah turned and left the bakery, the bell above the door tinkling again. As he stepped outside, he couldn't dismiss the feeling of being watched. Ruthie's harsh words echoed in his mind, making his chest tighten with frustration and hurt. He glanced around, but the street was empty. Pushing the thought aside, he walked briskly, needing to clear his mind and regain his composure.

His heart pounded with a mixture of anger and sadness as he tried to process Ruthie's reaction. The words stung more than he cared to admit. He had hoped she would understand or at least be patient. Instead, her sharp voice had cut deep, bringing back all the insecurities he had tried so hard to bury.

Isaiah found himself back at his buggy shop. The familiar smell of wood and metal greeted him, a comforting reminder of his purpose. He picked up a hammer, its weight in his hand grounding him. The rhythmic sound of metal on wood began to drown out the chaos in his mind.

The tools that fit his hands so well kept him busy enough to push Ruthie's attitude and look of frustration from his mind. Each precise movement, each carefully driven nail, allowed him to focus on something tangible, something he could control. The shop, with its organized chaos, was his sanctuary.

But the ache in his chest remained. He thought Ruthie was different... but maybe he'd never find a woman who would accept him for who he was. His constant need to move, his nervous energy, and the quirks that had always set him apart seemed insurmountable.

"Why can't things just be simple for once?" he muttered to himself, driving another nail into place.

As he lost himself in his work, the weight of his mission in Willow Springs felt a little lighter, though the uncertainty of his future with Ruthie remained. For now, he would focus on what he could control and hope that, in time, everything else would fall into place.

***

There was no denying she'd bothered Isaiah with her comment about his nervous energy. She could see the hurt in his eyes even though he tried to hide it. She'd seen that look before. It seemed that for every boy who ever came close, she'd let her sharp tongue and bossy attitude crush their spirit. She really hoped it would be different with Isaiah, but he was keeping secrets, and that made her doubt his sincerity. Couldn't she find a man who would be honest with her and accept her for who she was? Not like Samuel, who clearly had an agenda of his own. A man like Isaiah.

She was still beating herself up when Annie walked in the door carrying two milkshakes to share with her. Ruthie tried to put on a brave face, but the guilt gnawed at her, making it hard to hide her dismay from her best friend.

"Brought you a treat," Annie said with a cheerful smile, setting the milkshakes on the counter.

"Thanks," Ruthie replied, her voice lacking its usual enthusiasm. She took a sip, hoping the cool sweetness would soothe her frayed nerves.

"What's wrong, Ruthie? You look like you've got the weight of the world on your shoulders."

Ruthie sighed, looking down at her milkshake. "It's

nothing. Just... had a rough morning."

Annie frowned, not buying it. "Does this have anything to do with Isaiah? I just passed him, and he had the same look on his face."

Ruthie glanced up, surprised at how well Annie could read her. "*Jah*, I guess it does. I might have chased him away. I pointed out his quirkiness, and I think I hurt his feelings. I didn't mean to..."

Annie reached across the counter and interrupted her, placing a comforting hand on hers. "You've got to stop being so hard on yourself. Isaiah seems like a good guy. Maybe he needs some time to understand that you didn't mean any harm."

"I hope so," Ruthie muttered. "I'm just tired of pushing people away. I don't mean to—my mouth opens, and garbage comes out."

Annie decided to change the subject to lighten the mood. "You know, my *mamm* told me something interesting last night. When she was little, she heard a story of two forbidden lovers and the treasure they supposedly buried somewhere in Willow Springs."

"Really? Tell me more."

Annie leaned in, her eyes sparkling with excitement. "She

said the lovers used to hide clues all over town to meet in secret. The pinwheel design was one of those clues. Apparently, some old letters and diaries talk about their rendezvous spots. She thinks the treasure might be connected to those hidden places."

Ruthie wiped the condensation off her cup. "That's incredible. Do you think the recipe box, map, and the missing ledger are connected to those clues since they both have the same design?"

Nodding thoughtfully, Annie concurred. "It's possible. If we can piece together the clues, we might be able to figure out where the treasure is hidden. And who knows, maybe uncover some old secrets along the way."

Ruthie felt a spark of hope. "Isaiah also found a couple of clues that might lead us somewhere."

Annie smiled warmly. "What were they?"

Ruthie repeated what Isaiah had found as they sipped their milkshakes, adding another strange occurrence to their already long list.

***

Evert stood in the shadows near the library, his eyes fixed

132

on the bakery across the street. He watched as Samuel Glick and the two men who had been pursuing him entered the bakery, followed later by Isaiah and then Annie. His heart ached with longing as he observed their interactions, the camaraderie they shared, and the sense of belonging that he yearned for. But his past prevented him from getting too close to people. Until he could settle his debts, no one was safe.

His stomach clenched as he saw the two men who had been chasing him talking to Samuel. This wasn't the first time he had noticed Glick around and wondered what he was up to. He had seen him talking with Hilda and her sister Greta just the other day.

Evert leaned against the cold brick wall; his thoughts running at full speed. He missed the comfort of close friendships, the warmth of shared laughter, and the security of knowing he belonged somewhere. But his past mistakes had created a barrier, keeping him from forming new bonds. He had to stay distant to protect those he cared about, even if it meant enduring the loneliness that came with it.

His gaze shifted back to the bakery. Isaiah emerged while Ruthie remained inside, her silhouette visible through the window as she worked behind the counter. Evert couldn't help but feel a twinge of jealousy. Isaiah had managed to find a place in this community while he remained an outsider, lurking in the shadows.

As he watched Samuel and the two men, a sense of unease settled over him. Samuel had always been a sly character, and Evert couldn't erase the feeling that he was up to something. The fact that he was talking to the two men who had been hunting him only heightened his suspicion.

"What are you up to, Samuel?" Evert muttered under his breath. These men were dangerous, and if they were working with Samuel, it could only spell trouble for everyone in Willow Springs.

Evert's mind drifted back to the day he had seen Samuel talking with Hilda and Greta. They had seemed deep in conversation, their expressions serious. He wondered if they were all part of a larger scheme, one that involved the stolen recipe box, the missing ledger, and the old map. The pieces of the puzzle were starting to come together, but there were still too many unanswered questions.

He pushed off the wall and took a step forward, his eyes narrowing as he focused on the bakery. He had to find a way to protect Ruthie, Isaiah, and the rest of the community from the danger that lurked in the shadows. But to do that, he needed to uncover the truth and use the treasure to settle his debts once and for all.

With a measured breath, Evert retreated further into the shadows. He would continue to watch and wait, biding his time until the moment was right. He couldn't afford to make any mistakes.

***

Ruthie's heart pounded as she stood at the bottom of the attic stairs, the rush of hot air meeting her like a wave. It had been almost ten years since her mother had passed, but the attic, with its boxes and trunks filled with remnants of her mother's life, still held an air of mystery and nostalgia. She carried a flashlight, its beam cutting through the darkness, as she ascended the creaky stairs.

Her father had gone to a school board meeting, leaving her alone in the house. She felt a twinge of guilt for going behind his back, but the need to find her mother's diaries was too strong. Her father had always been adamant that those were their mother's private thoughts, and they had no right to disrespect her memory by going through them. He had even threatened to burn them, but he never had the heart to destroy all he had left of her.

Ruthie reached the top of the stairs, her flashlight illuminating the dust particles that danced in the stale air. She moved carefully, her eyes scanning the stacks of old trunks and boxes. She knew which trunks contained her mother's diaries from the time around her wedding and before. Her mother had always been a woman of secrets, and Ruthie was certain there were clues hidden within those pages.

She approached a large wooden trunk with her mother's initials carved into the lid. Her hands trembled as she opened it, the hinges creaking in protest. Inside, she found a treasure trove of memories—old letters and keepsakes. Ruthie sifted through them, feeling a mix of sadness and longing.

Finally, she found a stack of leather-bound journals, their pages yellowed with age. She picked up the one from around the time of her mother's wedding and opened it carefully. Her mother's elegant handwriting covered the pages, recounting the joys and challenges of her early married life.

As Ruthie read, she felt a connection to her mother she hadn't felt in years. The entries were thick with love, hope, and the occasional heartache. It was as if her mother were speaking to her from beyond the grave, sharing her most intimate thoughts and feelings.

Just as she was about to close the journal, something caught her eye; a passage that seemed out of place among the daily musings. It was a cryptic message, written in a different ink as if her mother had added it later: *"In threads of old, the past does dwell. Find the book that holds the tale."*

Ruthie's breath caught in her throat. This was the same message that had been engraved in the recipe box, she was sure of it. She knew this was another clue, one that would bring her closer to unraveling the mystery.

The distinctive sound of her father's buggy pulling into the driveway forced her to quickly close the journal and tuck it under her arm. She carefully sealed the trunk and made her way back down the stairs, her mind racing with possibilities. She had found what she was looking for and so much more. The clues were coming together, and she was determined to see this through to the end.

Ruthie slipped the journal into her pocket under her apron just as her father entered the house. She greeted him with a warm smile, trying to hide her excitement. She knew she would have to tread carefully, but she was more determined than ever to uncover the truth behind her mother's secrets and the mystery of the pinwheel design.

CHAPTER 8

Ruthie climbed into bed and spent most of the night reading through her mother's diary, her heart heavy as she felt her mother's heartbreak between the words. The entries had painted a picture of a young woman torn between duty and love, and Ruthie couldn't help but feel a deep connection to her mother's struggles. After only a few hours of sleep, dawn broke, but the pain of her mother's words still lingered in her room.

At breakfast, she nervously sipped her coffee, glancing at her father, who was engrossed in his morning paper. She took a deep breath, summoning the courage to speak.

"*Datt*, can I ask you something about *Mamm*?" Ruthie began, her voice tentative.

Her father's long graying eyebrows lifted at her request. "*Jah*."

Ruthie hesitated for a moment before continuing. "How did you and *Mamm* meet?"

A shadow crossed her *datt's* face, and he put the paper aside. "We met through an arranged marriage," he said slowly. "I grew up in a neighboring community, and our families arranged for us to be matched."

Ruthie leaned forward. "Oh… my. I didn't know that. Was that hard for both of you?"

He sighed; his gaze distant as if he were looking back through the years. "The initial years were troublesome because your mother's heart belonged to another. It was a tough time for both of us."

Ruthie's eyes widened in shock. "*Mamm* loved someone else?"

"*Jah*, she did. But eventually, our friendship turned into love. It took time, but we grew to understand and care for each other deeply."

Ruthie's mind raced with the implications of her father's words. Could her mother be the woman in the forbidden love story that Annie's mother had told her about? She wanted to ask more, but he quickly stood up, grabbed his hat, and added, "The plans we have for our lives aren't always the plans *Gott* has in store. Sometimes, His path takes us through trials and heartache to shape us into who we're meant to be."

Ruthie sat alone in the kitchen, long past the time she normally left for the bakery, pondering her father's words. They echoed in her mind, urging her to have faith in *Gott's* plan. If her father could marry knowing full well her mother loved another, how could she question *Gott's* plans for her own life? As she carried the breakfast dishes to the sink, she mumbled, "I'd rather be alone all my life than be matched with someone whose heart belonged to another."

***

No sooner had she unlocked the door to the bakery than Annie walked by heading to the Quilt Market. "Late morning?"

"*Ach*, I stayed up half the night reading through my mother's old diaries."

Ruthie took a calming breath as she pushed the door open and lifted the green shades. "I think my mother might be the woman in that forbidden love story your mother told us about. My father hinted at it this morning."

"Really? That would explain so much. Did he say who the other man was?"

Ruthie shook her head. "*Nee*, but my mother referred to him as a special friend with the initials HM. Her diary passages spoke of their two families—hers being hard-working farmers and his owning a successful business in town. For some reason, the two families didn't approve of their union and did everything they could to forbid their time together. HM finally gave in to his family's demands and moved to Mercer County, leaving my mother to mend her broken heart on her own."

"That's heartbreaking. It must have been so difficult for your mother."

A sad smile played on Ruthie's lips. "It explains a lot about why she was so reserved about her past. My father said their marriage was arranged, and it took years for their friendship to turn into love."

"I found something else in my mother's diary. There was an inscription inside the recipe box, and I found mention of it in my mother's entries. *'In the threads of old, the past does dwell. Find the book, the book that holds the tale.'* The recipe box was a wedding present with the first clue, long after HM left for Mercer County. It doesn't make sense that the clues would come after my parents married."

"So, the treasure hunt is connected to your mother's past and this HM. The book that holds the tale... Do you think it's one of your mother's old books or journals?"

Ruthie nodded slowly. "It must be. My mother kept detailed journals. If the recipe box was a wedding present, then HM might have left clues to guide her back to their shared memories or reveal something important."

Annie's mind raced with possibilities. "We need to find that book."

"I know. But I haven't seen anything else in my mother's journals from that time. This was the last entry about HM that I could find. Everything after this book was about my *datt* and us *kinner*."

Ruthie moved to the counter, set down her lunch and reached in her pocket to retrieve her mother's small journal. "Listen to this."

Dear Journal,

Today, I say goodbye to HM and the memories we created together. We both made our choices in life, and it is time for me to fully commit to Amos. I cannot live in the past any longer. My mother always told me to find joy in the season Gott has placed me in. So, I will not look back or too far forward. I will find joy in the present.

HM, I forgive you for making the choice you made, and I understand why you did it. I pray that someday, the clues we left for each other will lead others to understanding and peace. I will not follow the clues anymore. I will focus on my new life with Amos and build a future with him. May Gott guide us both on our separate paths.

With a heavy heart, Elsie

Ruthie choked up a bit as she read her mother's words. She could feel the pain and strength in her mother's decision to move forward. As she shut the diary, she realized that the treasure now held a different purpose. A part of her wanted to give up the hunt to preserve her mother's memory.

Protecting the memories her mother laid to rest some thirty years earlier seemed more important than unearthing old secrets. The treasure, once a symbol of mystery and adventure, had become a testament to her mother's past and the love she had chosen to leave behind.

"What now?" Annie asked.

Ruthie took a deep breath, trying to steady herself after the emotional moment. The reality of the situation settled over her like a heavy blanket, but Annie's words brought her back to the present. She placed the diary under the counter, and straightened up, her take-charge attitude resurfacing.

"I think we should just drop it all," Ruthie said, her voice firm but wavering slightly. "It's too much, and it's bringing up things that maybe should stay in the past."

"Ruthie, we can't just drop it. Someone is still stealing stuff that doesn't belong to them. We need to figure out how to stop it."

Ruthie sighed, glancing down at the diary. "So, what do you suggest we do?"

Annie leaned forward; her expression serious. "I think we need to talk to Isaiah. Maybe finding the treasure will stop all the speculation around town so things can return to normal."

Ruthie hesitated, her mind flashing back to Isaiah's hurt expression earlier. She was still unsure about his intentions and the secrets he was keeping, but she knew they couldn't solve this on their own.

***

Ruthie and Annie sat quietly in the Quilt Market after closing; Martha bustled about, tidying up the remnants of the day's activity. Sensing Ruthie's unease, she paused and offered a warm smile.

"Ruthie, what brings you here so late?" Martha asked, her voice gentle and inviting.

Ruthie hesitated for a moment before speaking. "I've been thinking a lot about my mother today. She died when I was so little, and I realize I don't know much about her. I know you were friends. Can you tell me more about her?"

Martha's eyes softened with understanding as she pulled up a chair and sat beside her. "Your mother would be so proud of you. She always wanted to own her own bakery, *jah* know? She used to say she had secret recipes that would make any bakery a success."

Ruthie smiled, longing for the mother she barely remembered. "She never got to live out that dream, did she?"

Martha shook her head, a hint of sadness in her eyes. "*Nee,* she didn't. When we were young girls, we worked in this very quilt shop together. Your mother had always dreamed of baking, and I had dreams of taking over my parents' quilt shop one day. She was so talented. Her fry pie secret filling recipes were legendary, even back then. They've certainly made your bakery a success."

Ruthie's heart swelled, but she couldn't let go of the feeling that there was more to her mother's story. "Did she ever mention a secret love? Someone with the initials HM?"

Martha's face turned thoughtful as she reminisced. "She always had her eye set on Herbert Miller. They were quite fond of each other, but Herbert's family wouldn't settle for anything but the best for their only son. She was so sure he was the one that she secretly worked on a special quilt for him, a beautiful piece with intricate designs. I'd forgotten all about it, but it was the pinwheel design, I'm sure of it."

"The pinwheel design?" Both girls said in unison.

"Do you know what happened to it?" Ruthie inquired.

Martha shook her head slowly. "I don't. One day, it came up missing, and she never mentioned it again. Soon after that, your father came along, and they got married."

Ruthie listened intently, her mind racing with the possibilities. "Do you think that quilt could be a clue in all this?"

Martha shrugged; her eyes distant. "I've always wondered what happened to it. But she moved on with her life, and so did Herbert. The quilt may hold some significance, especially with all these mysteries surrounding the recipe box and the pinwheel design."

Martha patted Ruthie's hand reassuringly. "Your mother was a remarkable woman. She faced many challenges, but she always found joy in the season *Gott* placed her in."

Ruthie felt a warmth in her chest, a connection to her mother that she had longed for all her life. "*Denki*, Martha."

As Ruthie left Annie and Martha in the Quilt Market, the cool evening air wrapped around her. She set out on the path to Isaiah's shop just as the sun's muted colors dropped below the horizon.

Her mind churned with Martha's revelations. The image of her mother, young and in love with Herbert Miller, filled her thoughts. She recalled Martha's words about the secret quilt and her mother's special recipes. Her mother had always dreamed of owning a bakery, a dream Ruthie was now living. But there was more to her mother's story than Ruthie had ever known. It felt like someone had left a breadcrumb, leading her towards something important.

Ruthie approached Isaiah's shop, her heart pounding since their last time together a few days earlier. She could see Isaiah through the window, busy at work. She felt a twinge of guilt for her earlier outburst.

Taking a steady breath, Ruthie knocked on the door, and Isaiah looked up, surprised but not unwelcoming. He waved her in through the window.

Gathering her thoughts, and without so much as a hello, Ruthie blurted out. "I've been piecing together more of the mystery. I just learned about my mother and a secret love, Herbert Miller. There's a quilt with a pinwheel design that she made that might hold more clues."

Isaiah's face changed at the mention of Herbert Miller, a flicker of recognition and something else passing over his features. It left Ruthie with another layer of questions.

Isaiah quickly masked his reaction and nodded. "That's a significant lead, isn't it?"

Ruthie responded, her eyes meeting his. "*Jah*. The recipe box had an inscription carved into it, and I found it written in one of my mother's diaries. '*In the threads of old, the past does dwell. Find the book that holds the tale.*' I think it's pointing us to something more."

Isaiah wiped his hands on a rag. "That's quite a clue. And it seems to tie in with what I found in the buggy shop. There's an inscription etched into an old table. Come see."

Isaiah led Ruthie through the shop back into his tiny

apartment and ran his hand over the aged carved words as he read. "'*Seek the harness that guides the way, where secrets lie, and history stays.*' They all have the same ring to them. Don't you think?"

He paused, glancing at her with a hesitant smile. "How about we discuss this over dinner? I'm hungry."

Ruthie hesitated, uncertainty flickering in her eyes. "Alright. Dinner sounds good."

***

Isaiah and Ruthie settled into a booth at the Restaurant on the Corner. The warm, inviting atmosphere was filled with the chatter of other diners and the soft clinking of cutlery. Ruthie couldn't help but feel a sense of anticipation. This was the first time she and Isaiah had spent time together outside of their shared quest to solve the mystery that had consumed their lives. Isaiah, who sat across from her, seemed just as nervous. His fingers fidgeted with a straw, folding and unfolding it precisely.

Ruthie watched him momentarily, a small smile playing on her lips as she observed his quirky habits. "Your hands always have to be busy, *jah*?" she asked gently, her tone more curious than critical this time.

He glanced up, his cheeks flushing slightly. "Helps me think and stay calm."

"Does it work"

With a sigh, Isaiah leaned back in his seat. "Sometimes. It's one of those things about me that people don't always understand."

Ruthie tilted her head, her appearance thoughtful. "It must be tough."

Isaiah shrugged, a faint smile tugging at the corners of his mouth. "It can be. I've learned to manage it, but it's not always easy. Sometimes, I feel like I'm too much for people."

As he spoke, he didn't notice the waitress standing nearby, waiting patiently to take their order. Ruthie glanced at the waitress, then back at Isaiah.

Ruthie smiled and added, "We all have our quirks."

Isaiah nodded, still oblivious to the waitress. "You know, you're different from other girls I've been around. You don't take any grief from people and are self-sufficient. It's a welcome change. I like your headstrong attitude... most of the time."

Ruthie chuckled. "Most of the time? I guess I've had to be strong growing up most of my life without a mother."

The waitress cleared her throat gently, and Isaiah finally looked up, realizing she was there. "We're ready to order."

Ruthie placed her order quickly, watching Isaiah as he fumbled slightly, clearly embarrassed. The waitress took their orders and left, and Isaiah turned back to Ruthie.

Isaiah saw a man sitting just over Ruthie's shoulder in a booth several seats away. His heart skipped a beat when he recognized him—the same man who had shown him Evert's picture. The man caught Isaiah's eye, and his eyes turned into a menacing glare. Isaiah's protective nature took charge, and he vowed to keep Ruthie safe.

He turned his attention back to Ruthie, trying to mask his concern. "What do you value in a friendship, Ruthie?"

Ruthie paused, considering the question. "Honesty. I value honesty above all else."

Isaiah's face shifted, a shadow passing over his features. He pulled back slightly, his fidgeting increasing. Ruthie noticed the change. "Isaiah, are you hiding something from me?"

Isaiah hesitated, his eyes darting away. He didn't want to put Ruthie in danger by revealing his involvement with Evert or the mystery surrounding his family. "There are things I can't talk about right now."

Ruthie's brow furrowed. "Isaiah, I need to know what's going on. If we're going to work together, there can't be any secrets between us."

Isaiah inhaled, struggling with his internal conflict. He wanted to protect Ruthie but didn't want to lose her trust. "Please, trust me a little longer."

Ruthie sighed, her heart aching with the weight of his words. She wanted to trust him, but the uncertainty bothered her.

Just then, Samuel walked into the restaurant, heading towards the two men Isaiah had been watching. Seeing Ruthie and Isaiah, he changed direction and slid into the booth beside Ruthie, interrupting their conversation. "Hey there, you two. Hope I'm not interrupting."

Ruthie forced a smile, hiding her annoyance. "Samuel, what brings you here?"

Samuel leaned back, looking far too comfortable. "I was just in the area and thought I'd check in. Have you heard any more about the thefts? It's troubling, isn't it?"

Isaiah's jaw tightened, and Ruthie could sense his irritation. "We're still trying to piece everything together, Samuel."

Ruthie felt her frustration boiling over. "Samuel, we're

trying to enjoy dinner. If you have something to say, say it."

Samuel raised his hands defensively. "Just making conversation. You know, families run deep in Willow Springs. If you look hard enough, you'll see old family secrets are hard to ignore."

Ruthie watched Isaiah's reaction to Samuel's comments, noticing the look of recognition, and her suspicion deepened.

Samuel's eyes narrowed, and Ruthie couldn't dismiss the feeling that he knew more than he was letting on. "What do you mean by that?" she asked.

Samuel shrugged. "Just saying, sometimes the past has a way of catching up with us."

Ruthie turned back to Isaiah as Samuel left, her thoughts tumbling over each other with questions, but Isaiah seemed a thousand miles away… lost in his own thoughts.

Isaiah watched Samuel walk away, his protective instincts flaring. He had to find a way to see his cousin without raising suspicion. The man's glare and Samuel's mention of family secrets left him wondering what he might know.

CHAPTER 9

Jedediah drove his delivery wagon through the peaceful streets of Willow Springs, the wheels creaking under the weight of his latest delivery. He glanced nervously in the back seat, where a copy of the stolen map lay concealed in a bulk food box. His heart pounded as he approached his destination, a farmhouse on the outskirts of town.

He pulled up and saw a shadowy figure waiting by the door. Keeping his head down, he climbed out of the buggy and walked over to the figure, clutching the box tightly.

The figure stepped forward, speaking in a low, stern voice. "Do you have it?"

Jedediah handed over the box. "It's inside."
The figure took the box and peered inside, confirming the map's presence. "Good."

Jedediah swallowed hard, his throat dry. "When do I get my money?"

The figure's eyes narrowed. "You'll get your money when we find the rest of the treasure. Not a minute before."

Jedediah's frustration bubbled up. "But I've already taken so many risks."

The figure's voice turned icy. "And you'll get it when I say so. Remember, you're in this just as deep as we are. The treasure is the key to everything."

Jedediah clenched his fists, feeling trapped. "Fine. But this had better be worth it."

The figure smirked a cold, calculating expression. "It will be. Keep your eyes and ears open and let me know if you find anything else. We're close, very close."

Jedediah nodded reluctantly, turning back to his buggy. As he drove away, he couldn't shake the feeling that he was being used. He needed the money desperately, but he also couldn't ignore the growing suspicion that he was in way over his head.

The shadowy figure returned to the farmhouse, clutching the map tightly in his hand. Once inside, he spread it out on a table, tracing the lines and symbols with his fingers.

A door creaked open, and another figure entered the room. "Did Weaver deliver the map?"

The first figure nodded. "Yes. He's desperate, but he'll do what he's told."

The second figure smiled. "Once we find the treasure, everything will fall into place."

The first figure frowned slightly. "What about the others? They're getting too close to the truth."

The second figure's smile faded. "We'll deal with them when the time comes. For now, we focus on the map and finding the treasure. Keep Weaver in line, and make sure he doesn't start asking too many questions."

They both studied the poorly made copy with sharp eyes, looking for any clue to the treasure's whereabouts.

***

Samuel trudged along the muddy path to Hilda's farmhouse, his frustration growing with each step. The spring rain poured down in heavy sheets, making the ground a slick mess. Mud caked on his boots, adding to the weight of his irritation.

Hilda stood on the porch, arms crossed and a scowl on her face as Samuel approached. She didn't bother hiding her disappointment when she saw the box in his hands.

"About time," Hilda snapped, eyeing the box suspiciously. "What took you so long?"

Samuel rolled his eyes, barely containing his annoyance. "I have better things to do than be your errand boy. I've got my own business to run."

Hilda's scowl deepened as she opened the box, her nose wrinkling in disgust. "These are stale! How am I supposed to perfect the recipe with days-old pies?"

Samuel's patience snapped. "You think I care about your baking experiments? I've been risking a lot to get those for you."

Hilda glared at him, her eyes becoming slits. "I need them fresh, Samuel. If you want this plan to work, you'll bring me what I ask for when I ask for it."

Samuel took a slow, deep breath, trying to regain his composure as the rain continued to pour, soaking through his coat. "Why are you so set on perfecting the recipe, anyway?"

Hilda's expression turned calculating, her eyes glinting with something darker. "You wouldn't understand. This is about more than just the recipes. It's about proving something—to myself and everyone else."

"You're hiding something. What's your real plan?"

Hilda's lips curled into a cold smile. "That's for me to know and you to follow through with. Just remember, we both have something to gain from this. Don't forget your place."

Samuel clenched his fists, his jaw tightening. He had a sinking feeling that Hilda was using him for her own ends, but he couldn't back out now. He was in too deep.

"Fine," Samuel muttered, turning to leave. "But don't push me too far. I'm not your lackey."

Hilda watched him go; her expression unreadable. She had a plan of her own, one that went far beyond perfecting Ruthie's recipes. This was about revenge for past hurts and reclaiming what Herbert and Elsie had stolen from her.

As Samuel walked away, his mind raced with thoughts of the treasure. He didn't care about Hilda's quest to steal Ruthie's customers; he only wanted the treasure and the wealth it promised. He needed to find it before anyone else, no matter the cost.

The rain continued to pour down, soaking Samuel to the bone. He slipped on the slick mud, barely catching himself before he fell. In the distance, Hilda's voice called after him, colder than ever. "Remember where your loyalties lie. You have more to lose than me."

***

The rain continued its relentless downpour, settling over Willow Springs in a gloomy gray. The bakery was quiet, with few customers braving the weather for baked goods. The usual hum of activity was replaced by the rhythmic drumming of rain bouncing off the windows and the occasional creak of the old building.

Ruthie sat at one of the small tables near the window, her mother's diary in front of her. The words blurred as she tried to focus, her mind racing. She needed answers, and she hoped her mother's diary might hold the key.

She flipped through the pages, stopping at an entry dated six months before her parents' wedding. The handwriting was neat but urgent, the words hinting at a deep and painful secret.

June 15, 1980

I can hardly bring myself to write this, but my heart is heavy with the burden of what I've heard. A lie so devastating that it could shatter any hope for a future with HM. The words whispered in the shadows have planted a seed of doubt and fear in everyone who's heard. Jealousy and anger have festered for years, and now they've turned into a rumor I can't face.

If they believe the rumor, then there is no hope for us. I must tell the truth, but I am terrified of what it might do. I can't even write it down for fear of the inevitable heartbreak.

Ruthie's hands trembled as she read the entry. She could feel her mother's anguish, the weight of the secret that had threatened to destroy her future. The mention of jealousy and anger struck a chord, and Ruthie's mind raced to piece together the puzzle and what her mother might be referring to.

She closed the diary, staring out at the rain-soaked street just as Isaiah bolted into the bakery, the heavy rain soaking through his coat and dripping onto the floor. He didn't even notice the mess he was making as he shook the rain from his hat, his mind too focused on the chart he tucked under his coat to keep dry.

He'd spent hours compiling the clues and mapping out their connections, and he was eager to show Ruthie his work.

"Ruthie!" he called out, his voice filled with urgency and excitement. "I've got something to show you!"

Ruthie looked up from the table where she had been poring

over her mother's diary. Her irritation flared as she saw the puddles forming around Isaiah's feet. "Isaiah, you're dripping all over my floor!"

He glanced down, realizing for the first time the mess he was making. "Oh, I'm sorry," he said, taking a step back, but the excitement in his eyes didn't wane. "I'll clean it up, but first, you need to see this."

Ruthie grabbed a mop from the corner. "Alright, let's see what you've got."

Isaiah unfolded the chart, spreading it out on the table. "I've been piecing together all the clues we've found," he explained, his fingers tracing the lines and notes he'd drawn. "There are still some gaps in our information, but I think we're getting close."

After Ruthie mopped up the water and put the mop away she sat down, her irritation giving way to curiosity. "Alright, show me what you've got."

Isaiah's eyes lit up as he began to explain. "So, the recipe box had the first clue: '*In the threads of old, the past does dwell. Find the book, the book that holds the tale.*' We haven't found the ledger yet, so that's the first gap."

Ruthie's eyes followed Isaiah's hand as he pointed to

various notes on the chart. "And then there was the clue inside the buggy shop: *'Seek the harness that guides the way, where secrets lie, and history stays.'* That led us to the harness shop, and the clue on the back of the frame. *'The key you hold, the map's path shows. Beneath the bench, treasures glow.'*"

Isaiah continued. "And then there was the park bench riddle: *'Where the pinwheel turns and shadows meet, go to the spot where secrets greet.'* We haven't figured out where that points yet either."

Ruthie leaned closer. "So, what does it all mean?"

Isaiah took a gulp of air. "I think it means that all these places are connected by a common history—a history involving your mother, and possibly others. The clues are leading us to something big, something hidden in Willow Springs that ties all these threads together."

Ruthie's mind raced, trying to piece everything together. "It's starting to make sense now. But we still need to figure out how it all connects to my mother, Herbert Miller, and the Millers' old family secrets."

Isaiah nodded. "Exactly. And there's more to it than just finding the treasure. We need to understand why these clues were left and what they mean."

Ruthie's mind wandered back to the conversation she had with her father about her mother's past and the forbidden love story and why he was so adamant about keeping her mother's memory at peace. "But what could it be? And why would someone go to such lengths to hide it?"

Isaiah shook his head. "I'm not sure yet, but I think we're getting closer to finding out."

Isaiah then pointed to another section of the chart, where he'd listed all the people who seemed interested or involved. "We have to consider the people who might be involved. There's the man showing the picture around town. Samuel, who's been acting suspiciously. Hilda, with her strange obsession with your bakery. And Eleanor Fischer, the historian who seems to know more than she's letting on."

Ruthie stared at the chart, the weight of her mother's secrets and the mystery they were unraveling pressing down on her. "And then there's this." She opened her mother's diary and pushed it over so Isaiah could read the entry about a secret that upset her mother.

He took a few seconds to read the entry. Then, his fingers fidgeted with the edge of the chart. "There's something else I need to tell you."

Ruthie tipped her chin in his direction and waited.

He took a deliberate breath, meeting her gaze. "HM—Herbert Miller—is my uncle. He died over twenty years ago, and I think he might be the HM your mother has referred to. My family always said he died of a broken heart. He never married and never had children."

"Herbert Miller? Is that the secret you've been keeping from me?"

Isaiah replied slowly. "I didn't see how it all might fit until you found your mother's diary, and the initials matched. I'm unsure if it's just a coincidence, but I thought you should know."

Ruthie's mind raced with the implications of Isaiah's words. The mystery was deepening, and the connections between their families were becoming more intricate.

Isaiah looked down; his expression distressed. "We need to figure out how all these pieces fit together."

As they sat together, poring over the chart and discussing their next steps, the rain continued to pour outside, its steady rhythm reminding them they were still missing so many clues.

Ruthie stopped and looked at the chart again. "You don't have the two men I saw on the street. And the man who came into the bakery asking questions. I can't help but think they're all involved somehow."

Isaiah picked up the pen and added him to the chart. Quietly, however, he hoped Evert wasn't a suspect.

***

Later that afternoon, the rain finally let up, leaving the streets glistening under the late afternoon sun. The scent of wet earth and blooming lilacs hung in the air as Ruthie stepped out of the bakery, taking a moment to breathe in the moist, post-rain air. She glanced around, her eyes landing on Isaiah, who was sitting on the bench across the street, his eyes focused on the old wooden park bench where he had found one of the clues.

Feeling a flutter in her chest, Ruthie crossed the street and joined him on the bench. "Hey," she said softly, her voice cutting through the quiet of the evening.

Isaiah looked up, a smile spreading across his face when he saw her. "Taking a break?"

She nodded, sitting down beside him. "Yeah, the bakery's been slow with the rain and all. Thought I'd come out and enjoy the fresh air."

Isaiah chuckled, running a hand through his damp hair. "I was just thinking the same thing."

Ruthie glanced at him, noticing how his eyes sparkled with excitement despite their challenges. "You're really into this mystery, aren't you?"

Isaiah's face turned serious. "*Jah*. But it's not just about the treasure or the clues. It's about understanding the past, connecting our families, and maybe even finding closure to these riddles."

Ruthie smiled, touched by his words. "I get that. I've learned so much about my mother through all this."

They sat in comfortable silence for a moment, the sounds of the town slowly returning as people ventured out after the rain.

Isaiah nodded in the direction of the building across the street. "There's something about this bench placement that feels important."

Ruthie glanced around, looking intently at the building across the street. "What are you looking so hard at?"

As they sat there, Ruthie detected Isaiah's eyes shifting to the Quilt Market across the street. Above the shop, she saw an old, faded quilt design that resembled a pinwheel.

"Look at that," he pointed out. "The design above the Quilt

Market. I've noticed a faded shadow on the side of my building. Like a metal sign or something hung there, leaving the wood underneath not faded by the sun. I didn't realize it before but it's the same design."

Ruthie turned to him, intrigued. "Do you think it's part of the puzzle?"

Isaiah nodded; his mind a hive of activity. "I think so. I've always loved puzzles. I can't keep focused on too many things all at once, but I pick up on things quicker than most people. Like that shadow on the side of my buggy shop that matches the design above the Quilt Market."

Ruthie's admiration for Isaiah grew as she listened to him. They sat in silence again, their connection growing stronger with each passing moment. Ruthie felt a sense of peace she hadn't felt in a long time, and she realized that despite the chaos and mystery surrounding them, she was starting to fall for Isaiah.

"Ruthie," Isaiah said softly, breaking the silence.

"*Jah?*" she replied, turning to look at him.

"I... I like you," he admitted, his voice filled with vulnerability. "I just wanted you to know." And with that, he quickly stood and walked away, leaving Ruthie on the bench, wondering if she'd heard him correctly.

***

Evert peered out the window of the *Sandwich Shoppe*, his eyes fixed on Isaiah and Ruthie as they sat on the park bench across the street. Memories of his childhood flooded his mind, mixing with the present reality. He remembered playing with Ruthie in the schoolyard, their laughter echoing through the fields. Those were simpler days, filled with innocence and joy, before his father uprooted the family and moved them to a much stricter community north of Willow Springs.

The rain had finally let up, but the streets glistened with the aftermath of the downpour. Evert took a deep breath, rubbing the scar on his chin as memories flooded his mind as he watched the two of them together.

Years earlier, Evert had been part of a troublesome trio. He, along with two other men, had formed a small gang that caused havoc in the neighboring towns. The night he got his scar was still vivid in his mind. They had been on the hunt for clues, convinced that Ruthie's house held something valuable, a key to an old family secret they had been chasing for years.

"Are you sure this is the place?" one of the men whispered, his eyes darting around nervously.

"Yes, this is it," Evert whispered.

They made their way to the side of Ruthie's house, the darkness of the night cloaking their movements. As they approached the window, Evert felt a pang of guilt. He didn't want to break into Ruthie's home. She had been a friend before everything went wrong.

"Let's just get what we need and go," Evert urged.

The other man was less cautious. They'd brought a crowbar, and they started prying it open as soon as they reached the window. The sound of splintering wood made Evert wince.

"Stop," he had hissed. "You're going to wake someone up!"

"Relax, we know what we're doing."

Evert's heart had raced as he watched them work. Just as they were about to break the window, Evert heard a noise behind them.

"Who's there?" a voice had called out.

Evert's panic surged. He turned to see old man Mast standing in the doorway, his eyes wide with shock. Without thinking, Evert lunged, keeping his friend from going after Ruthie's father.

"What are you doing?" the old man hollered.

In the chaos that followed, Evert had been struck by the crowbar. The pain was immediate and intense, a searing burn across his chin. He had fallen to the ground, blood dripping down his face.

"Let's get out of here!" he yelled, running into the night. Shortly after that night, they had all been arrested for robbery. It had been years since that fateful evening, but the scar on his chin was a constant reminder of his failure to protect the town that held so many fond memories.

Evert snapped back to the present; the memory still fresh in his mind. His gaze softened as he watched Ruthie laugh at something Isaiah said. The harsh reality of his current life seemed to melt away, replaced by the warmth of those long-gone days.

But the memories were quickly overshadowed by the bitterness of his past decisions. Running away, turning to crime to survive, losing the security and love of his family, it had all led him to this moment.

He sipped his coffee, trying to focus. He needed to talk to Isaiah. The sooner they unraveled the family secret, the sooner he could put all this behind him and finally find, his peace.

As Isaiah stood up from the bench and said his goodbyes to Ruthie, Evert gulped down the rest of his coffee and followed, keeping to the shadows and blending in with the town as best he could.

Evert trailed Isaiah a safe distance behind, his heart pounding with anticipation. He needed to know what Isaiah had figured out about the family mystery. It was their only chance to set things right.

Meanwhile, Ruthie stayed on the bench, her thoughts swirling with the emotions stirred by her conversation with Isaiah. She needed to understand what he'd said and how his words had affected her. After a few minutes, she stood up and followed Isaiah, needing clarity and answers.

As Ruthie approached the buggy shop, she saw Isaiah enter. She was about to call out to him when she noticed a figure slipping in behind him. Her heart skipped a beat as she recognized the man from the bakery—the same man who'd been asking questions and making her uneasy. She pressed herself against the side of the building, peering around the corner to watch.

Inside the shop, Isaiah was startled to find Evert had

followed him inside. "Evert," he said in a low voice, closing the door behind him. "What are you doing here?"

Evert looked around nervously, ensuring they were alone. "I had to talk to you. I need to figure this out, and fast. I can't keep hiding like this."

Isaiah nodded. "I've been working on it. The clues are making sense, but we need more time."

Making her way just short of the open door, Ruthie listened intently, her anger rising as she realized Isaiah was keeping yet another secret. The man they had been looking for—the man who had caused so much turmoil—was right there in the buggy shop, and Isaiah had known who he was all along.

Evert's voice trembled slightly. "I can't go on like this, Isaiah. The longer this drags out, the more danger I'm in."

Isaiah placed a reassuring hand on Evert's shoulder. "We'll figure it out. But we need to be careful. Ruthie and the others can't be dragged into this."

Ruthie clenched her fists, her heart pounding. She had to confront Isaiah and the strange man and demand the truth. Taking a profound breath, she stepped out from her hiding place and pushed open the door to the buggy shop, ready to face whatever came next.

CHAPTER 10

Taking a deep breath, Ruthie swung the door open and stepped inside, her eyes narrowing at the sight before her. "So, this is it? Another secret you've been keeping from me?" she spat, glaring at Isaiah and Evert.

Isaiah looked up, his eyes wide with surprise and guilt. "Ruthie, what are you doing here?"

"I should be asking you that," she snapped, crossing her arms over her chest. "Who is he, Isaiah?"

Evert tried to step forward, but Ruthie's fierce glare stopped him in his tracks. "Stay out of this. I don't even know who you are, and I don't care to find out," she said, her voice shaking angrily.

"Look harder, Ruthie. You know me," Evert snapped.

Ruthie's eyes narrowed as she scrutinized him. The scar on his chin and his short hair threw her off, but there was something familiar in his eyes. Memories of a childhood friend began to surface, someone who had always been by her side during school, before he and his family suddenly left.

"Evert?" she whispered, the realization dawning on her. "Evert Miller?"

"Yes, it's me," Evert said, stepping forward cautiously.

Ruthie looked hard as she took in the transformation. The years had changed him, but the essence of the boy she once knew was still there. "I can't believe it's you," she said, her voice softening for a moment before the anger returned. "But that doesn't explain why you're here, and why Isaiah kept this from me."

Isaiah's face was flushed, his fingers twitching nervously. "Ruthie, please, let me explain. It's not what you think."

"Not what I think?" Ruthie laughed bitterly. "How can I have confidence in you when you keep so many secrets?"

Isaiah reached out to her, but she stepped back, shaking her head. "Don't. Just don't. I don't want to hear any more excuses. I thought you were different, Isaiah. But you're just like everyone else."

"Ruthie, this is Evert, my cousin," Isaiah said, his voice trembling. "We're both Herbert Miller's nephews. Evert's been in hiding, and I didn't want to drag you into this mess."

She turned on her heel and stormed out of the shop, slamming the door behind her. Isaiah stood there, staring at the closed door, feeling a deep sense of loss. He wanted to run after her, to make her understand, but he knew it was too late. Ruthie needed time, and he had to respect that.

Evert placed his hand on Isaiah's shoulder. "I'm sorry, Isaiah. I didn't mean to cause so much trouble for you."

***

Hilda and Greta braved the heavy rain as they drove their old buggy to the bulk food store for supplies. The rhythmic clopping of horse hooves against the muddy road was accompanied by the constant drumming of rain on the buggy's roof. Hilda held the reins tightly, her face set in a determined expression, while Greta sat beside her, her hands folded in her lap, her thoughts distant.

The gloomy weather did little to improve their moods. Hilda's mind was a whirlwind of thoughts and plans. She couldn't shake the unease that had settled over her since Samuel's visit. Her frustration with him and the situation gnawed at her, but she kept her composure.

As they approached the store, Greta broke the silence. "Hilda, do you think we have enough money for all these supplies?"

Hilda glanced at her sister, her expression softening for a moment. "We should. If not, Jedediah can easily be convinced to offer us credit."

Greta turned her eyes downcast. "I suppose so."

The rain continued to pour as they arrived at the bulk food store. Hilda tied the horse to the post, securing the buggy. The rain showed no signs of letting up as they hurried inside, shaking off the dampness from their clothes.

Inside the store, they were greeted by Jedediah, the owner, who offered them a guarded smile. "Braving the storm, I see." Hilda nodded curtly. "We need supplies."

Greta, ignoring her *schwester's* internal struggle, chatted with Jedediah about the latest news in the community. Hilda's mind, however, was elsewhere, planning her next move and how to stay one step ahead of anyone who might threaten to uncover her secrets.

When they finished their shopping, Jedediah helped them load the supplies into the buggy. As they prepared to leave, Hilda leaned in close to Jedediah, her voice barely a whisper.

"Remember, our agreement."

Jedediah's face tightened, his nervousness more apparent. "I haven't forgotten."

Hilda's eyes narrowed, her voice dropping even lower. "Good. And remember, there's no turning back now."

Jedediah swallowed hard, glancing around as if worried someone might overhear them. "I know. It's just... I never imagined it would go this far."

Hilda's face hardened; her eyes boring into his. "Neither did I."

Standing a few feet away and distracted by the rain, Greta missed the whispered exchange. Hilda straightened up, ensuring her sister hadn't noticed anything amiss. As they climbed back into the buggy, Hilda couldn't help but mutter, "Driving this buggy in the rain is such a hassle. Sometimes, I think cars would be so much easier."

Greta looked at her sister, shocked by the bold statement. "Hilda! What a thing to say."

Hilda quickly composed herself, her face a mask of determination. "I know, Greta. It was just a thought. I remember having fun driving during my rumspringa. Let's get home before the rain gets any worse."

Back at the bakery, Hilda sat down with her notebook and reviewed her notes on the filling for Ruthie's fry pies. She had nearly perfected the recipe, and the filling tasted almost identical to Ruthie's. A smug smile tugged at her lips. All she needed now was to get the local customers to know that her baked goods were as good or better than Ruthie's.

Greta entered the kitchen, hanging up their wet shawls. "Hilda, do you really think this will work?"

Hilda's eyes gleamed with determination. "Once the word spreads that our baked goods are just as good, if not better, than Ruthie's, we'll get our customers back. And then, we'll finally get what is rightfully ours."

Greta's face was etched with worry. "I hope you're right. I don't want any more trouble."

As they worked together in the kitchen, Hilda couldn't shake the feeling of satisfaction. She had gotten so close, and nothing would stop her now. She would see her plans through, no matter the cost.

***

Later that evening, Ruthie stood at the stove, frying pork

chops. The comforting aroma of simmering fat and roasting vegetables filled the kitchen, but her mind was far from the task at hand. She was still reeling from the confrontation with Isaiah and Evert. She had stormed out of the buggy shop, her emotions a whirlwind of anger, betrayal, and confusion. Now, the silence of her home seemed both a comfort and a burden.

Her father sat at the kitchen table, reading the evening paper. The headline about the attempted bank robbery caught his eye, and he frowned as he read. "Did you see this article about the bank robbery? The robbers weren't after money but something in one of the safe deposit boxes."

Ruthie glanced over; her curiosity piqued despite her inner turmoil. "Something in a safe deposit box? What could be so important?"

"I don't know, but it's strange, isn't it? You'd think they'd go after the money."

Ruthie's thoughts returned to the tangled mess of her own life. "*Jah*, strange. But there's been a lot of strange things happening around here lately."

Amos looked over his glasses perched low on his nose. "Are you alright? You seem troubled."

Ruthie forced a smile. "Just tired, I guess."

After dinner, Amos retired to bed, leaving Ruthie alone with her thoughts. She cleaned up the kitchen, her movements mechanical and slow. Once the dishes were done, she wandered onto the porch, seeking solace in the cool evening air.

She settled into one of the old rocking chairs, pulling a shawl around her shoulders. The night was quiet, save for the distant croak of frogs and the rustle of leaves in the breeze. She rocked gently, her mind replaying the events of the day.

She thought about Isaiah and the look of hurt in his eyes when she confronted him. She had been so angry, so ready to lash out, that she hadn't given him a chance to explain. And now, sitting alone in the dark, she felt a pang of regret.

But the revelation about Evert and Isaiah's secret had shattered her trust. She had hoped for something different with Isaiah, something real and honest. Yet the secrets and lies had only confirmed her deepest fear—that she would always be alone.

Tears welled up in her eyes as she hugged the shawl tighter around her. The prospect of a future without companionship, without love, weighed heavily on her heart. She had tried to be strong, to be independent, but in moments like this, the loneliness was almost too much to bear.

She looked up at the sky, the stars twinkling in the vast expanse above. "Why, *Gott*?" she whispered, her voice breaking. "Why can't I find someone who's honest and true? Why does it always have to end like this?"

The night offered no answers, only the gentle sway of the rocking chair and the quiet symphony of the countryside. Ruthie wiped her tears away, determined not to let despair take root. She had to be strong, for herself and for her father.

But deep down, the pain lingered, a reminder of the hopes dashed and the dreams unfulfilled. As she sat there, rocking back and forth, Ruthie resolved to keep moving forward, no matter what the future held.

***

Eleanor Fischer sat in a corner of her kitchen, surrounded by stacks of old records and documents. The faint hum of the fluorescent lights and the occasional snore from her husband in the other room were the only sounds in the otherwise silent room. Eleanor's eyes were strained from hours of searching, but she was intent to find the missing pieces of the puzzle that had eluded her for so long.

Her persistence finally paid off when she stumbled upon an old family Bible neatly tucked away in a box she had purchased at an estate sale. The fragile paper crinkled as she carefully unfolded it, tracing the lines and names with her finger. As she read through the entries, her eyes widened with realization. There it was, in faded ink—Evert Miller and Herbert Miller were indeed related, and more surprisingly, Isaiah King was related to them.

Eleanor leaned back in her chair; her mind was a whirlwind of activity with the implications. The tangled web of relationships was beginning to make sense, and a slow smile spread across her face. This newfound knowledge was a significant breakthrough, and she was committed to use it to her advantage.

But Eleanor's motives were far from pure. She had spent years following the Miller family's trail, driven by a personal vendetta. Her family had a history intertwined with the Millers, one filled with betrayal and loss. She harbored a deep resentment towards them, believing that her family had been wronged many years ago.

As she gathered her papers, Eleanor's thoughts turned dark. She recalled the stories passed down from her mother—the whispers of a hidden treasure, a family fortune that had slipped through their fingers that should have been hers. She had grown up with tales of this treasure, and now, with the connections she had uncovered, she felt closer than ever to finding it.

Eleanor's mind flashed back to her childhood, remembering her mother's hushed tones and the bitter edge in her voice whenever she spoke of the Millers. "They took everything from us," she would say, her eyes hard with unresolved anger. "One day, you'll make it right and find a way to get back what was taken from us."

Determined to fulfill her mother's wishes, Eleanor had dedicated her life to unearthing the truth and reclaiming what she believed was rightfully hers. The Miller family's secrets had become her obsession, and she had sacrificed much in her relentless pursuit.

With the Bible safely tucked into her bag, Eleanor left the kitchen, her mind buzzing with plans. She needed to stay one step ahead of Ruthie and Isaiah, using the information she had gathered to manipulate the situation to her benefit. She knew she had to be careful; one wrong move could unravel everything she had worked so hard for.

She knew she had to find a way to use the knowledge of the

family connections to her advantage, to turn the tides in her favor. The tangled relationships between Evert, Herbert, and Isaiah were the key to unlocking the treasure and exacting her revenge.

Eleanor's thoughts were interrupted by a sudden rumble of thunder. She pulled her sweater tighter around her as her mind raced with possibilities. The hidden treasure was within reach, and she would stop at nothing to claim it.

Back in her small, cluttered bedroom, Eleanor spread out the documents on her bed, studying them with a meticulous eye. She scribbled notes in the margins, connecting dots and forming strategies. The Miller family's past was laden with secrets and lies, but she was confident she could navigate it.

Just as she was about to dive back into her research, her husband entered the room. His face was etched with frustration.

"You've been obsessed with this treasure hunt for years. It's taking over your life. When will you let it go?"

Eleanor looked up from her papers. "I'm so close. I found an old family tree that proves Evert Miller, Herbert Miller, and Isaiah King are related. This could be the breakthrough I've been waiting for."

"And what does that change? You've spent countless hours

and money chasing this treasure. We hardly spend any time together anymore. You're always buried in your research."

"You don't understand. This isn't just about the treasure. It's about reclaiming what was stolen from my family. My mother always said they took everything from us. I have to make it right."

Her husband's shoulders sagged. "But at what cost, Eleanor? Our marriage? Your sanity? Please, just consider letting it go."

"I can't. Not when I'm this close. I found an old German Bible at an estate sale. It outlines the genealogy of the local Miller family. There are clues in there that could lead us to the treasure."

He threw his hands up in defeat and left the room. Eleanor turned back to her documents and determined the treasure and the retribution she sought were within her grasp.

***

Samuel sat in his workshop, the steady hum of his tools and the rhythmic tapping of his hammer providing a soothing backdrop to his thoughts. The rain had finally let up, leaving the night silent and still. His focus was fixed on the piece of wood in front of him—a new recipe box he was crafting for Ruthie. Without the original as a pattern, he was relying entirely on his memory.

The pinwheel design had him concentrating the hardest. The pattern was a familiar one throughout Amish country. He'd seen it countless times, even noting a quilt with that pattern hanging on the wall at Greta's quilt shop. It was a design etched into his mind, yet replicating it perfectly required precision and care.

As he worked, Samuel's thoughts drifted back to his childhood. He had always liked Ruthie, even as a boy. But now, with Isaiah King showing interest, Samuel felt a surge of possessiveness he hadn't expected.

He berated himself for being so consumed with building his construction business that he had given little thought to Ruthie until Isaiah started hanging around. There was something oddly familiar about Isaiah King that Samuel couldn't quite put his finger on. He had an air about him, something that stirred old memories and nagged at the edges of Samuel's mind.

One thing Samuel knew for certain: he wasn't about to let Isaiah get to Ruthie's heart before he did. He was adamant about winning her over, to prove that he was the right choice. Ruthie needed someone who understood her and had known her for years, not some outsider with a quirky personality.

He carved the intricate details of the pinwheel pattern, his mind racing with thoughts of how to win Ruthie over. The scent of freshly cut wood filled the workshop as he finished the final touches on the box. He stepped back, admiring his work. The recipe box was beautiful, a testament to his skill and his feelings for Ruthie.

He would deliver the box to Ruthie in the morning, and with it, a piece of his heart. He was ready to fight for her, to prove that he was the man she needed. Besides, he was Samuel Glick, and he wasn't about to let anyone take what he believed was rightfully his.

***

The next morning, Samuel set out early to deliver the newly crafted recipe box to Ruthie. The sky was overcast, a hint of rain still lingering in the air, and the streets of Willow Springs were just beginning to come to life. He carried the box carefully, his heart pounding with a mix of anticipation and arrogance.

Ruthie was opening the bakery when Samuel arrived. She looked up, her face still showing the remnants of the emotional storm she had weathered the day before. Her eyes were puffy, and she moved with a heavy heart. Seeing Samuel, she forced a small smile, trying to muster the energy to greet him.

"Morning, Ruthie," Samuel said, his voice warm but with a hint of his usual cocky attitude. "I brought you something." Ruthie looked at the box in his hands and felt a mix of emotions.

Samuel handed her the box, watching her closely. "I made you a new recipe box. I know it's not the same as the one you lost, but I thought it might help."

Ruthie took the box, running her fingers over the intricate pinwheel design. She was touched by the gesture, but the pain of losing the original box still lingered. "It's beautiful. But it's not just the box I miss. It's the recipes. They were my connection to my mother."

Samuel shrugged, trying to dismiss her sentiment. "Recipes are just a bunch of ingredients. You can make new ones."

"Well, it's done now. Maybe this new box can hold new memories for you. Besides, I'm sure you can develop even better recipes."

Ruthie managed a weak smile. "Maybe. But it's hard to let go of the past."

Samuel replied in a tone that was more dismissive than understanding. "You can't live in the past forever, Ruthie. You must move on."

Ruthie looked at him, a hint of frustration in her eyes. "It's not that simple, Samuel. Some things are worth holding on to."

Samuel smirked, his arrogance shining through. "If you say so. Anyway, I hope you appreciate the box. It wasn't easy to make without the original to go by."

Ruthie felt a pang of guilt. "I do appreciate it, really."

Samuel leaned on the counter. "How's your new friend, Isaiah? Have you heard anything more about him?"

Ruthie's expression darkened. "Actually, I've been thinking you might be right about him. He's been keeping secrets, and I don't know if I can trust him."

Samuel's smirk widened. "I had a feeling about that guy. You should be careful. Some people aren't what they seem."

Ruthie nodded, her frustration growing.

As they stood in the quiet bakery, the air filled with the scent of yeast, Samuel felt a surge of satisfaction. He had planted a seed of doubt in Ruthie's mind about Isaiah, and that was exactly what he wanted. He couldn't let anyone else get close to her, especially not someone like Isaiah.

"Well, I've got to get going," Samuel said, turning to leave.

Ruthie watched him go, a mix of suspicion swirling in her mind. She appreciated the gesture of the recipe box, but something about Samuel's demeanor didn't sit right with her. She couldn't shake the feeling that he was hiding something as well.

CHAPTER 11

Isaiah wiped the sweat from his brow as he secured the new buggy wheels. The old shed smelled musty, a mix of damp wood and stale air that clung to his clothes. As he stepped back to admire his work, he saw Hilda approaching, her normal scowl etched across her brow.

Hilda tipped her head toward the newly installed wheels. "These should last a good while, *jah*?"

Isaiah smiled as he handed her the bill. "You should be good for a long while."

"Follow me to the bakery, and we'll settle. You can sample some of our new recipes if you'd like."

Isaiah hesitated for a moment, not liking how the mention of 'new' recipes sent up a red flag for him.

Hilda's expression turned forceful, almost snarling. "You must try one of our new fry pies. They're the best in town."

Isaiah raised an eyebrow at her intensity but nodded. "Of

course, I'll take one of each."

As he walked out of the shop, Hilda called after him, "Make sure you let us know what you think. We're confident you'll be impressed."

Isaiah forced a smile and nodded again, but as he walked away, he couldn't shake the feeling that something was off. Hilda's eagerness was too much, and the way she had snarled about the new recipe made him wonder what she was up to. It was odd how she was purposely pushing the fried pies.

On his way back to town, Isaiah contemplated stopping at Ruthie's bakery. He needed to find a way to talk to her, and the fry pies he picked up would give him a good reason to stop. Besides, he wanted to make amends and prayed he hadn't angered her so badly she wouldn't even to talk to him.

***

When Isaiah arrived at Ruthie's bakery, he was met with a wary nod that quickly turned into a look of confusion.

"You stink. Why do you smell like moldy hay?"

Isaiah chuckled nervously. "Sorry about that. I was working in Hilda and Greta's old shed. It's musty in there."

Ruthie wrinkled her nose but accepted the box of baked goods. "What's this?" she snarled. Her wariness evident on her face, her demeanor turning cold. "Why are you really here, Isaiah? Still keeping secrets?"

Isaiah sighed. "I'm trying to make things right, Ruthie. I know you're upset with me, and you have every right to be. But I thought you might want to know that Hilda was fixated on making sure I knew her recipes were new. It made me wonder what she was up to."

Ruthie raised an eyebrow, opened the box, and poked her finger into each one. "Lemon? Raspberry? And chocolate?" Ruthie's eyes narrowed. "New recipes, huh? Let's see." She picked up one of the fry pies, taking a cautious bite. Her eyes widened, and she gasped. "This is my recipe!"

She grabbed one of her own fry pies from the display case and took a bite of each, comparing the flavors. "They're identical. Hilda stole my recipes. I'm sure of it."

Isaiah watched as Ruthie's anger grew. She took the other raspberry and chocolate from the box and compared the flavors. Each one was a perfect match to her own recipes.

In the middle of her furious taste testing, Annie walked in. "What's going on here?"

Ruthie thrust a fried pie at her. "Taste this and tell me what you think."

Annie took a bite. "This tastes just like yours." She examined the bakery box. "How did Hilda get your recipes?"

Ruthie fumed. "That's what I need to find out. I think I'll go ask her myself."

Annie put her arm around Ruthie, trying to calm her down as she paced back and forth in the small bakery. "You need to calm down. Confronting Hilda face to face won't solve anything. It might even make things worse."

"I can't just sit here and do nothing! She stole from me, and she's trying to ruin my bakery!"

Isaiah stepped forward; his voice steady but gentle. "Annie's right. You should let Detective Powers handle this. He has the authority to investigate and get to the bottom of it. If you confront Hilda now, it could jeopardize everything."

Ruthie clenched her fists, her anger simmering just below the surface. "Fine. But if he doesn't do anything, I will."

With a sigh, Annie said. "Call Detective Powers and let him know what we've found."

After Annie left, the bakery felt tense and heavy. Isaiah

lingered, unsure how to approach the topic weighing on his mind. "Can we talk about Evert?"

Ruthie shot him a cold look. "I don't care what you're up to with Evert. I only care about saving my bakery and getting my mother's recipes back."

Isaiah's scrutiny shifted to the new recipe box on the counter, and jealousy flared in his chest. "Where did that come from?"

Ruthie's eyes hardened. "Samuel made it for me. He's been more helpful than you've been."

"I don't trust him." Isiah snapped.

Ruthie's voice was sharp. "That goes both ways, and he doesn't trust you either."

Isaiah's frustration bubbled over, and he began fidgeting, his fingers tapping nervously on the counter. "You don't understand. There's more going on here than you realize."

Ruthie crossed her arms. "Then help me understand and stop hiding things from me."

Isaiah opened his mouth to speak, but the words wouldn't come. He felt trapped, knowing that revealing too much could put them all in danger. "I can't. Not yet."

Ruthie's eyes flashed with anger. "Then leave. I don't need

your help if you can't be honest with me."

Isaiah's shoulders slumped, the weight of her words pressing down on him. With a nod of farewell, he turned to leave and added, "I'm trying to protect you. Whether you believe it or not."

As he walked out of the bakery, the door closing behind him with a sharp clang, Ruthie's anger gave way to a pang of regret. She watched him go. A part of her wishing things could be different but unable to shake the feeling of betrayal.

Alone in the bakery, Ruthie tried to refocus her thoughts on the task at hand. She needed to get her recipes back and prove that Hilda was behind the thefts. As much as she wanted to believe in Isaiah, the secrets he was keeping made it impossible. And with Samuel's constant presence, the lines between friend and foe were becoming increasingly blurred.

Isaiah stepped out of the bakery and onto the sidewalk, the warm air hitting his face. He had hoped his conversation would ease the tension, but all it did was make things worse. He needed to find a way to regain her trust. Resolving to clear the air, he changed his mind about telling her the truth and pushed back open the bakery door.

Ruthie looked up from behind the counter, her expression still frosty. "Isaiah," she acknowledged curtly, her voice edged with irritation.

"Ruthie, please," Isaiah began, his voice earnest. "I need you to understand everything that's going on. Can we talk after the shop closes tonight? I'll bring Evert, and we'll explain everything."

Ruthie hesitated, her eyes narrowing with suspicion. "Why should I meet with Evert? He's part of the reason I don't trust you."

Isaiah nodded, accepting her wariness. "I know, and I don't blame you. But please, give us a chance to explain. It's important. We need your help to solve this and to keep everyone safe."

Ruthie studied him for a moment before sighing. "Alright. But if I feel like you're still hiding something, I'm done!"

Isaiah's face softened with relief. "Thank you. I'll see you later."

***

Later that evening, Ruthie flipped the closed sign on the

bakery door and pulled the blinds down. She took a cleansing breath, trying to steady her nerves. Just then, a knock sounded at the back door. She opened it to find Isaiah standing there with Evert.

"Come in," Ruthie said, stepping aside to let them in. She locked the door behind them and turned to face the two men.

Evert looked around the bakery, his expression a mix of nostalgia and regret. "Thank you for agreeing to meet with us, Ruthie."

Ruthie crossed her arms, her gaze unwavering. "Start talking."

Evert took a drawn-out breath, his eyes meeting Ruthie's. "I know you have every reason to distrust me, but I need you to understand what's been happening." He shifted his weight and leaned back on the counter. "When I was young, I made a lot of bad decisions. I got mixed up with the wrong crowd—the same two men who are chasing me now. They're after the treasure, and they'll stop at nothing to find it first."

Isaiah stepped forward, his voice steady. "Evert begged me to help. He doesn't deserve it, but I couldn't turn my back on him… he's family."

"Our uncle, Herbert Miller, loved your mother deeply."

Every began, "He hid clues all over town, leading her to a hidden treasure, showing his love for her. But someone spread a horrible lie about them, which forced Herbert's parents to send him away to prevent him from tarnishing their name."

"My mother wrote about Herbert in her diary. She gave up all connections to him and devoted herself to my father. She was heartbroken."

Evert crossed his arms over his chest. "But my mistakes brought others into this. They discovered the treasure through me and are now hunting for it."

Ruthie's face softened slightly, and she looked at Isaiah. "Is this the secret you've been keeping from me?"

Isaiah nodded decisively. "*Jah*, and I'm sorry I didn't tell you sooner. My father encouraged me to settle this once and for all. I'm good at solving puzzles, and if there's any truth to this treasure, we want to find it first to honor our uncle Herbert."

Ruthie tried to process everything. "So, what do we do now?"

Evert's voice was firm. "We need to work together to solve these clues and find the treasure before they do. It's the only way to protect everyone. The men who are chasing this treasure will do anything to get what they want, and it won't matter who gets in their way."

Isaiah nodded. "Each stolen item is another clue pointing us to the treasure's location. Without all the clues, the location remains a mystery. People have been trying to discover the whole series of clues for the past thirty years."

They sat down and began to piece together the clues, hoping to get closer to the hidden treasure. Evert explained how he was trying to change his life but couldn't do so with his old friends hot on his trail.

Ruthie suddenly remembered something Martha had told her. "Martha mentioned that my mother made a quilt for Herbert, but she never knew what happened to it. I think the ledger might hold the location of that quilt."

With a firm nod, Isaiah agreed. "It's possible. We need to find that ledger."

As they continued to talk, Ruthie noted Isaiah's scent again. "You smell. Hilda needs to fix that old leaky roof; the odor penetrates everything."

Evert's eyes widened with recognition. "I know that smell. I've smelled it before, but I can't place where it's from." Evert leaned back in his chair, and added, "It's a memory that I can't quite grasp."

Isaiah became agitated, a sudden realization hitting him. "The two men who tried to rob the bank... they had that same smell. I noticed it when I was chasing them."

Evert's eyes flickered with recognition and shock. "Yes! The last time I saw those men, they had that same musty smell on them. It was just a few weeks ago."

Ruthie's face grew pale as she pieced it all together. "Hilda must be working with those two men. The same men who tried to rob the bank were chasing Evert."

Isaiah frowned, his mind working quickly. "But what would they be after at the bank?"

Evert hesitated before speaking, his voice low. "Uncle Herbert had a safe deposit box at that bank. I bet that's what they were after."

"How would they know that?" Ruthie asked.

A sudden shame covered Evert's face. "I'm sure I mentioned it in one of my drunken states."

"Regardless, the real issue is what Hilda has to gain by being involved in this."

***

Hilda stood near a stall at the Willow Springs Farmer's Market, her eyes darting around as she spotted familiar faces. With a determined smile, she approached a group of women chatting animatedly.

"Good morning, ladies," Hilda said, her voice dripping with false sweetness. "Have you heard about Ruthie's bakery?"

One of the women looked up curiously. "What about it, Hilda?"

Hilda lowered her voice conspiratorially. "Well, I heard she's been having some trouble keeping her recipes straight. A few customers told me her latest batch of fry pies was a bit off. Imagine, losing the touch so soon."

The women exchanged concerned glances. "That's surprising. Ruthie's always been spot on with her flavors."

Hilda nodded, feigning sympathy. "It's such a shame. Maybe she's just overwhelmed. Running a business isn't easy, you know."

She leaned in closer, her voice dropping to a whisper. "And did you hear about the incident last week? Someone found a hair in one of her fry pies. Quite the health concern, don't you think?"

The women gasped, their eyes widening with shock and shaking their heads. "Oh dear, that's terrible. I hope it was just a one-time mistake."

Hilda's expression was one of fake concern. "I hope so too. But you know how these things go. One bad experience can really damage a business's reputation."

As Hilda walked away, she couldn't help but feel a twisted satisfaction. The seed of hesitation had been planted, and she relished the thought of Ruthie's customers second-guessing their loyalty.

She glanced back over her shoulder, watching the women whisper among themselves. Hilda walked away, holding her head high. Her plan to ruin Ruthie's reputation was unfolding perfectly.

***

Ruthie stood behind the counter, wiping down the spotless surface for the third time that hour. The doorbell tinkled as a couple of customers left, empty-handed. She glanced at the clock. Business had been unusually slow all week.

Annie held the door open for the leaving customers and walked up to the counter. "What's going on? It's so quiet in here."

Ruthie shrugged, trying to mask her worry. "I don't know. It's been like this for days."

"I heard some whispers at the market this morning. Hilda was talking about how she's got some old family recipes with unique ingredients. She also made some not-so-subtle comments about your inexperience."

"Of course she did. That old biddy has been after my business for years. But why would people believe her?"

Annie placed a reassuring hand on Ruthie's arm. "We know your baking is the best. We just need to remind everyone else."

Ruthie's frustration bubbled inside her. "I need to confront Hilda. I'm certain she took my mother's recipes. It's the only thing that makes sense." Ruthie pulled out a tub of flour and set it on the worktable. "I called Detective Powers, but since we don't have any hard evidence, there wasn't much he could do but take down the information."

Annie squeezed Ruthie's arm. "Maybe we need to gather more evidence first. If we can prove she stole the recipes, Detective Powers will have to act."

Ruthie's determination replaced her frustration. "You're right. But I'm not going to let Hilda get away with this. My mother's recipes mean everything to me. I'll do whatever it takes to get them back."

Annie's eyes twinkled with a new idea. "Why don't you beat her at her own game? Come up with some new flavors. Fry pies are your biggest seller, but there are other flavors you could create."

"That's a great idea, Annie. I'll start experimenting right away. If Hilda thinks she can outdo me, she's got another think coming. She can spread all the rumors she wants, but I'll show everyone what I'm made of."

Annie smiled. "That's the spirit!"

"But I'm still not going to let it lie. I think I might just visit Hilda's bakery on my way home tonight. I need to set some things straight."

***

Ruthie walked into Hilda's bakery, her eyes scanning the room. The scent of baked goods wafted through the air, but Ruthie's attention was immediately drawn to a quilt hanging on the wall with a familiar pinwheel design. Her heart skipped a beat.

"Hilda," Ruthie called out, trying to keep her voice steady.

"Nice quilt you have there."

Hilda turned, her smile faltering slightly. "It's an old family heirloom."

Ruthie stepped closer; her eyes fixed on the quilt. "The pattern is familiar. My mother made a quilt with a similar design years ago. Do you know where this one came from?"

Hilda's eyes darted nervously. "Oh, it's been in the family for years. I'm not sure of its exact origins."

"Really? Because it looks a lot like the one my mother made for Herbert Miller."

Hilda's face tightened, and her voice dropped to a cold, threatening tone. "I don't know what you're implying, but I have work to attend to. And I'd advise you to be careful with your accusations."

Ignoring Hilda's dismissal, Ruthie pressed on. "And about the recipes for your fry pie filling. I know my mother's recipes, and the ones you've been using taste the same. Did you steal them?"

"You have no proof of that. Accusing me of stealing is a serious matter, and you'd better watch yourself. I've been in this business far longer than you, and I won't have my reputation tarnished by some young upstart."

Ruthie held her ground, her voice unwavering. "I may not have proof yet, but I will find it. My mother's recipes mean everything to me, and I won't let you get away with this."

"Good luck with that, Ruthie. You're in over your head. Now, if you'll excuse me, I really do have work to do."

Ruthie took in Hilda's reaction. "Of course. I'll see myself out."

As she turned to leave, Ruthie couldn't shake the feeling that she was onto something. The quilt, Hilda's nervousness, and the taste of her fry pies all pointed to a deeper connection. But what Hilda was up to was beyond her.

***

Ruthie left the bakery and as the door swung shut behind her, Greta emerged from the back room, wringing her hands. "I overheard your conversation," Greta said, her voice trembling. "Are you sure we should be doing this? What if she finds out the truth about the recipes?"

Hilda's face hardened, and she turned to face her *schwester*. "Greta, don't start with your nervous babbling. We've come too far to turn back now. Those recipes are ours now, and she can't prove anything."

"But…" Greta insisted, her voice dropping to a whisper, "What about those two creepy men? They're on the back porch right now, waiting to talk to you. I don't like this. It's getting too dangerous."

"Those men are necessary for our plan, Greta. They're helping us find the rest of the treasure. And since they messed up the whole bank deal, they owe us."

Greta bit her lip, her anxiety evident. "I just don't want anyone to get hurt, Hilda. I distrust those men."

"We're in too deep to back out now," Hilda snapped. "We must see this through, for our sake and for the bakery. Now, go make sure everything is in order in the kitchen. I'll deal with the men."

With a reluctant nod, Greta retreated to the back room.

Hilda steeled herself for the meeting. She couldn't afford to let anyone see her fear or doubt. The stakes were too high, and she was determined to come out on top, no matter the cost.

She walked to the back door and opened it, revealing the two men waiting on the porch. Their expressions were cold and calculating, sending a shiver down Hilda's spine.

CHAPTER 12

Isaiah was sanding a newly constructed buggy wheel in the workshop when he heard the door creak open. He glanced up to see Noah standing there, looking more serious than he had ever seen him.

"Noah, what brings you here?"

He stepped inside, closing the door behind him. "I found something embedded in the back of the map frame."

"What do you mean?"

Noah pulled a small, worn key from his pocket. "It looks like a key to a safe deposit box."

Isaiah took the key, turning it over in his hand. "And you think this box holds a clue?"

Noah nodded. "It must. Why would it be hidden on the back of the map unless it holds a clue to the map?"

Noah sat down on a nearby stool, a weary look crossing his face. "Isaiah, there's more you need to know. My parents told me some stories last night about Ruthie's mother and Herbert Miller. There were lies spread among Willow Springs, causing tension between the Millers' and Ruthie's mother's family."

Isaiah frowned. "Lies? What kind of lies?"

Noah sighed deeply. "Terrible ones. There were rumors about Herbert's intentions and about Ruthie's mother's character. No one ever knew who spread them, but they created a wedge that seemed impossible to remove. The lies made it look like Elsie was pursuing Herbert for his family's wealth and that she was unfaithful. It poisoned everything."

Isaiah cleared his throat. "How could someone be so cruel?"

Noah shook his head. "Those lies led to Herbert and Elsie being torn apart. Herbert's family sent him away, and by the time he discovered the truth, it was too late. Ruthie's mother had married Amos, and the damage was done."

"We need to find the rest of the clues and stop this stupid game once and for all." Isaiah replied.

"That's why I brought you the key."

Isaiah gripped the key tightly. "I'll go to the bank first thing in the morning."

***

Isaiah and Ruthie sat still in the small, private room at the bank, the key to the safe deposit box lying on the table between them. The air was thick with anticipation and the low hum of the bank's operations outside the room.

Evert stood in the corner, his eyes darting between Isaiah and Ruthie. His old selfish desires flickered in his eyes, anticipating a treasure that would change his fortunes. Ruthie and Isaiah, however, were united in their pursuit of the truth.

Ruthie's hands trembled slightly as Isaiah inserted the key and turned it. The box opened with a soft click, revealing a stack of old papers, a small gold key, and a worn leather journal.

Isaiah carefully lifted the journal, his fingers brushing over the aged leather. "This must be it," he whispered, opening the book to the first page. Herbert Miller's familiar handwriting greeted them, his words a poignant reminder of the past.

As they turned the pages, they found sketches and notes detailing places around Willow Springs, where he left messages meant only for Elsie's eyes. But it was the mention of the Old Mill that caught their attention: "*Where dawn breaks, the truth awaits. Behind tools rest, the path is best.*"

Ruthie's eyes widened. "The old mill… we need to go there at dawn. That's where the truth will be revealed."

"But there's more. Look." He turned to a page that held a folded letter, yellowed with age. Carefully, he opened it, revealing a heartfelt message from Herbert to Elsie.

My Dearest Love,

As I sit on our favorite bench, I'm overwhelmed by the sorrow that fills my heart. The lies that were whispered tore us apart and left scars that may never heal.

I cannot undo the past, but I can leave you my heart and all that I have. This key will unlock our treasure, and you'll find not only my words, but everything I had hoped we would share together. What was meant to be our future now belongs to you alone. Use it as you see fit, for I cannot bear to enjoy it without you.

I leave you my heart, my treasure, and my eternal love. May you find happiness, even if it is without me. And if you ever doubt my love, look to the dawn at the old mill. There, the truth will be drawn.

Forever yours,

Herbert

Tears welled up in Ruthie's eyes as she read the letter aloud.

The sorrow and love in Herbert's words touched her deeply, a testament to the pain and longing that had marked their lives.

As they carefully placed the items back in the safe deposit box, a sense of determination filled the room. They were not just uncovering the past; they were setting things right and bringing closure to a love story that had been left unfinished for far too long.

***

Samuel paced the narrow alley behind Main Street, his footsteps echoing off the brick walls. The dusky April sky was dipping below the horizon, and the air was filled with the pungent smell of newly manured fields. The twilight added a touch of magic to the scene, but Samuel's mood was anything but light. He checked his watch for the third time, frustration growing with each passing minute. Finally, a buggy pulled up beside him, and Hilda glared at him, her face twisted in a sneer.

"You're late," Samuel snapped, his voice low and angry.

Hilda raised an eyebrow, unimpressed. "I don't appreciate being summoned like this, Samuel. You're forgetting who holds the cards here."

Samuel took a step closer, his expression dark. "I've done what you asked. I stole the recipe box, delivered the recipes, and even made sure Ruthie's bakery took a hit. I want my payment, Hilda."

Hilda's eyes narrowed, a cold smile playing on her lips. "And you'll get it when the time is right. Don't forget, you're not the only one with something at stake here."

Samuel's hands clenched into fists. "I'm tired of waiting. I took all the risks, and you're reaping the benefits. How do I know you'll hold up your end of the deal?"

"Because if you don't stop pestering me, I'll make sure Ruthie knows exactly who's been behind all her troubles. Do you really want her to find out you've been working against her all along?"

Samuel's eyes flickered with fear and anger. He opened his mouth to retort, but she cut him off, her tone icy. "I've seen the way you watch her at church. It's quite clear what your true feelings are. Imagine how she'll feel when she discovers that you betrayed her. That you were the one who stole her precious recipes and handed them over to me."

Samuel's face reddened. "You wouldn't dare."

Hilda chuckled, the sound chilling in the narrow alley. "Try me. You've done your part, and you'll get what's coming to you. But don't think for a second that you can dictate terms to me."

Samuel turned away, muttering under his breath. "This isn't over, Hilda."

"Oh, I know it isn't, Samuel. Not by a long shot."

Samuel needed to find a way out of this mess, a way to make things right without destroying any chance he had with Ruthie. But for now, he was stuck, caught in Hilda's web, and the only thing he could do was wait for the right moment to strike back.

***

Ruthie and Isaiah stood in the dimly lit buggy shop, the scent of wood and metal mingling in the air. They had been going over the latest clues, trying to piece together the puzzle that had consumed their lives. Suddenly, Isaiah glanced out the window and froze.

"Is that... Samuel?" Isaiah asked, his voice low and cautious.

Ruthie moved closer to the window, peering out into the alley. There, in the fading twilight, she saw Samuel pacing back and forth, his movements agitated.

"What's he doing here?" she asked.

Before Isaiah could respond, a brown-topped buggy pulled up beside Samuel, its wheels crunching on the gravel. They watched as Samuel's stance changed, his posture becoming more guarded. The person inside the buggy didn't get out, remaining shrouded in shadows.

"Who is that?" Ruthie whispered, her heart pounding. Isaiah shook his head, his eyes narrowing as he observed the buggy. "I can't tell. But whatever they're discussing, it doesn't look good."

They both strained to hear, but the distance and the soft hum of the evening made it impossible. All they could see was Samuel gesturing animatedly toward the buggy.

They waited until the conversation in the alley seemed to end. The buggy slowly started to pull away, and Samuel watched it leave before heading in the opposite direction.

"Isaiah, did you recognize the buggy?" Ruthie asked softly. Isaiah nodded, his mind working quickly. "Look at the wheels, Ruthie. See those distinct markings on the spokes? I made those wheels myself a few weeks back. And that brown canvas top— it's new. I fixed it for Hilda not long ago."

Ruthie's eyes followed Isaiah's direction, taking in the unique features. "You're sure it's her buggy?"

"Positive," Isaiah said, his voice firm. "There's a small patch on the left side of the canvas, near the rear corner. Hilda had a tear there, and I mended it for her. Plus, the way the horse is hitched, Hilda always uses that particular bridle setup. It's definitely her buggy."

Ruthie's mind raced, trying to piece together what this meant. "Why would Hilda be meeting with Samuel?"

"I don't know," Isaiah admitted, "but it can't be good."

***

Jedediah sat in his dimly lit office, the scent of musty old papers and ink permeating the air. His bulk food store was barely staying afloat, and the stress of it all weighed heavily on him. Hidden beneath a pile of ledgers and invoices was his forbidden cell phone, a device he had to keep secret from his church district, which forbade its use.

The phone buzzed softly, and Jedediah glanced around nervously before picking it up. "Meeting tonight. Usual spot."

Later, Jedediah made his way to the secluded meeting spot,

his heart pounding. Hilda's two *Englisch* friends, who had been pressuring him for weeks, were already there, their faces obscured by the dim light.

One of the men stepped forward, his eyes glinting with malice. "We saw Evert Miller, Ruthie Mast, and Isaiah King go into the bank together. We're certain they have information we need. We need you to get it."

Jedediah's stomach churned. "You want me to break into *Isaiah's Buggy Shop*? I don't think I can do that. It's too risky."

The second man grabbed Jedediah by the collar, pulling him close. "Listen, Weaver, you're in this just as deep as we are. If you don't help us, we'll make sure the police find out you have a copy of the map on your phone. That'll link you to the break-in, even if you didn't steal the map yourself."

Jedediah's mind raced. He had no choice. He had to find a way out of this mess. "Alright, alright. I'll do it. But this is the last time. I'm done after this."

The men released him, smirking. "Just make sure you get what we need. Or else."

Back at his store, Jedediah sat down, trying to piece together his next move. He knew he had to be careful. One wrong move, and his whole world could come crashing down worse than just the financial mess the store was in.

***

The late-night air was cool and crisp, the soft hum of crickets and the occasional rustle of leaves the only sounds that broke the silence. Isaiah and Ruthie sat on a bench outside the buggy shop, the dim glow of the shop's lantern shining a warm light around them.

They had just witnessed Samuel's suspicious behavior in the alley and were now deep in thought, processing the implications. Ruthie looked up at the stars, the vast expanse of the night sky calming her nerves.

"It's amazing, really," she said, breaking the silence. "How our families were connected all those years ago and now, here we are, crossing paths again. What do you think it means?"

Isaiah looked thoughtful, his fingers fidgeting with a piece of straw he had picked up. "I'm not sure. Maybe it's *Gott's* way of giving us a chance to set things right. To mend old wounds and find closure."

Ruthie's no-nonsense demeanor softened slightly. "You might be right. It's just... strange how things work out."

Isaiah glanced at her, a nervous twitch in his hands. "Do you really believe that? That *Gott* has a plan for all of this?"

Ruthie shrugged. "I've always believed in *Gott's* plan. It's just that sometimes, it's hard to see the bigger picture."

Isaiah's fidgeting intensified, and he looked away, his gaze fixed on the ground. "You know, I've always struggled with... well, with being different. My ADHD, my quirks... I've never felt like I fit in. I talk too much, I can't sit still, and it feels like I'm too much for people to handle."

Ruthie turned to face him; her expression sincere. "Everyone has their quirks. I'm bossy and blunt, and I've scared off more suitors than I can count. I didn't think I'd ever find someone who could put up with me."

Isaiah chuckled softly, finally meeting her eyes. "It's hard to imagine you scaring anyone off."

Ruthie laughed. "Oh, trust me, I have. But you know what? I think maybe that's why we understand each other. We've both got our... oddities, but maybe that just makes us a better match."

Isaiah's twitching subsided. "You really think so?"

"I do. We might be a little much for other people, but maybe we're just right for each other."

CHAPTER 13

The quilt shop was a haven of color and warmth, with quilts hanging on the walls and fabrics neatly stacked on shelves. The soft light filtering through the windows gave the room a cozy, welcoming feel. Ruthie entered the shop; her thoughts were darting in every direction with the discovery she had made a few days earlier. She found Martha busy organizing a stack of fabrics, her movements precise and practiced.

"Martha, I need to talk to you," Ruthie said urgently, her voice trembling slightly.

Martha looked up, concern in her eyes. "What's wrong, Ruthie?"

"I visited Hilda's bakery the other day and saw a quilt with a pinwheel design hanging on the wall. It looked exactly like the one you described my mother made for Herbert."

"Are you sure?" Martha asked, her brow furrowing.

"I'm certain. When I mentioned it, Hilda got all nervous."

Martha's brow furrowed. "That quilt disappeared years ago. If it's the same one, it could be a significant clue."

"What should we do?" Ruthie asked, her voice filled with determination.

Martha sighed; her gaze distant as she considered their next steps. "If it's the quilt I helped your mother work on, I'll recognize it." Martha recounted the past. "I remember when your mother made that quilt for Herbert. There was always a bit of tension between her and Hilda. Hilda once had eyes for Herbert, and there was no love lost between them."

Ruthie listened intently, her mind piecing together the fragments of the past. "Do you think Hilda could have taken the quilt out of jealousy?"

Martha shrugged. "It's possible. Hilda was always determined to get what she wanted, and your mother was her rival in many ways."

"Why would Hilda have it?" Ruthie asked, frustration tinging her voice.

Martha shook her head. "I don't know, but we need to find out."

They sat in silence for a moment, pondering their next move. Martha's eyes lit up as an idea formed. "I think I'll find an excuse to visit Hilda's bakery. Maybe I can ask Greta about some old quilt patterns or something. While I'm there, I'll take a closer look at that quilt."

***

The tension in Willow Springs had reached a boiling point. Bishop Schrock called for a special meeting at the school, urging all church members to attend. The air was thick with unease as families filed into the small, one-room schoolhouse. The recent break-ins had shaken the community, and the threatening message left behind had only heightened their fears.

Bishop Schrock stood at the front of the room, his presence commanding respect. He raised his hand for silence, and the murmurs gradually subsided. "Brothers and sisters, we're facing troubling times. The recent break-ins and thefts have unsettled our community, and we must come together to address these issues calmly."

He glanced at Detective Powers, who stood off to the side, a reassuring presence. "I've invited Detective Powers here to help us. I know some of you feel that we should handle this matter within our community, but we must consider every option to protect our families and our way of life."

Detective Powers stepped forward; his expression serious yet empathetic. "Thank you, Bishop Schrock. I understand your concerns and respect your desire for privacy. However, the threats and break-ins have escalated, and it's clear we need to work together to find a solution. I'm here to offer my assistance and ensure your safety."

The room buzzed with whispers as families exchanged worried glances. Isaiah and Ruthie sat together; their expressions grim. The break-in at Isaiah's buggy shop had only revealed a message scrawled in red paint on the wall that was still fresh in their minds: *Leave the past buried before it's too late.*

Isaiah stood up, his voice steady as he tugged his collar and tried to remain in control of his quirky tics. "My shop was broken into, and while nothing was stolen, the message left behind was clear. They're targeting us, and we need to find out who is behind this."

Detective Powers nodded. "I've seen these tactics before. They're trying to instill fear in the community. We need to remain calm and vigilant. Has anyone seen anything unusual or suspicious?"

An older man, Mr. Zook, raised his hand. "I saw a couple of strangers hanging around the shop late last night. They didn't look like they belonged here."

Bishop Schrock frowned. "We need to stay united and look out for each other. If anyone sees anything suspicious, report it immediately."

After the meeting, Ruthie and Isaiah stood outside the schoolhouse, the cool evening air a stark contrast to the heated discussions inside. The sky was painted with the soft hues of twilight.

Ruthie turned to Isaiah; her eyes filled with a glimmer of hope. "We can't let them scare us away. We must find out who is behind this."

Isaiah's gaze steadied.

Ruthie felt the weight of the recent weeks pressing down on her shoulders. "We need to talk to everyone, find out if there are any more clues. Maybe someone saw something they didn't realize was important."

As they walked back to Isaiah's buggy, the bond between them grew stronger with each step. Ruthie glanced at Isaiah, her heart swelling with gratitude. She was happy to have him near, to have someone to lean on and share the burden of the mystery that had engulfed their lives.

"I'm glad we're in this together," Isaiah whispered.

Ruthie blushed slightly, her cheeks warming in the cool air. "Me too."

They reached the buggy, and Isaiah helped Ruthie up, his touch gentle and respectful. As he climbed in beside her, he felt a sense of peace, knowing she was beside him.

The ride back was quiet, the rhythmic clip-clop of the horse's hooves soothing their minds. Ruthie leaned back, allowing herself to relax for the first time in days. The darkness outside was a blanket of security, wrapping them in a cocoon of shared purpose and growing affection.

When they arrived at Ruthie's house, Isaiah helped her down from the buggy. She paused for a moment, looking into his eyes. "Thank you, Isaiah."

Without saying a word, he brushed his finger against her cheek and let it linger on her lips for just a second before climbing back inside.

"Good night, Ruthie," he replied, his voice filled with warmth.

As she watched him drive away, she touched her lips, still warm from his touch, and smiled. A real heartfelt smile she hadn't allowed herself to enjoy for a long time.

***

The next morning, Ruthie and Isaiah set out to speak with their neighbors. The break-ins and threats had created a sense of urgency, and the community was more united than ever.

At the Lapp family farm, Mrs. Lapp offered them tea and a listening ear. "We've heard about what's been happening. If there's anything we can do to help, just let us know."

Ruthie smiled gratefully. "Thank you, Mrs. Lapp. We're trying to piece together any information that might lead us to the culprits." Ruthie took a sip of her tea and continued, "We believe this all has something to do with my mother and Herbert Miller. You and my mother were friends, right?"

The older woman smiled tenderly. "*Jah*, Elsie was a dear friend of mine."

"Is there anything you might remember that could help us?" Isaiah asked.

"All I can say is I give your father a lot of credit. He had to endure the rumors for years... long after the two of them married. It takes a special kind of man to marry a woman whose name has been dragged through the mud like your mother's was."

Mr. Fischer, an elderly man with a deep knowledge of the town's history, shared his memories with them. "I remember when Herbert Miller was a young man. He was always talking about hidden treasures and secrets. He was a big talker, so I never paid too much attention to the stories that floated throughout Willow Springs long after he left. Just hearsay I'd say."

Isaiah listened intently, his mind racing. "Thank you, Mr. Fischer. Any information could be valuable."

Mrs. Stoltzfus, a woman in her late seventies, said, "There were always rumors about the Miller family and the Mast family. Some said they were cursed because of forbidden love. Herbert and Elsie were the talk of the town. It was said that lies and jealousy kept them apart."

Ruthie's eyes widened. "Do you know who spread those lies?"

Mrs. Stoltzfus shook her head. "No one ever knew for sure. But whoever it was caused a lot of pain for both families."

As the day went on, Ruthie and Isaiah visited more families, each conversation bringing them closer to understanding the bigger picture.

That evening, they returned to the bakery, exhausted but determined. "I have to believe that whoever spread those rumors thirty years ago has to be the one who is still trying to cause trouble today."

"I agree," Isaish added. "If we can figure out who stirred up this mess between our families, I bet we'll find the root of our problem.

"But what about the treasure?" Ruthie asked. "How does the treasure fit into the rumors and lies that forced my mother and Herbert apart?" Ruthie sank into her chair and rested her chin in the palm of her hand. "Nothing makes sense."

***

The sounds of the lumber mill pervaded the environment with a constant hum of activity—saws buzzing, logs thudding, and workers shouting instructions. Ruthie walked through the bustling yard, her heart pounding as she approached the office where her father was busy overseeing the day's work.

She found him leaning over a stack of paperwork, his face lined with age and weariness. At sixty, he was still a strong man, but the years had taken their toll. His once-steady hands now trembled slightly, and his eyes held a perpetual look of sadness.

"*Datt*," Ruthie called softly, trying to catch his attention over the noise of the mill.

Amos looked up, annoyance flickering in his eyes. "Shouldn't you be at the bakery?"

"I needed to talk to you," she said, stepping closer. "It's important."

Amos set down his pen and leaned back in his chair. "What's on your mind?"

Ruthie's heart was heavy with the questions that had been plaguing her. "I've been learning more about *Mamm* and her relationship with Herbert."

Amos's face hardened, his expression darkening. "Why do you want to dredge up the past, Ruthie? Some things are better left buried."

"But I need to understand. There are too many unanswered questions. People are talking, and I need to know what really happened."

Amos's eyes flashed with anger. "Your mother's name doesn't need to be dragged through the mud. Herbert is dead, and so is your mother. Let them rest in peace."

"I found out that someone spread rumors about *Mamm* and Herbert. Who would do such a thing?"

"It doesn't matter who did it. What matters is that your mother chose me, not him. She made her choice, and we built a life together."

"But the past is affecting the present," Ruthie pleaded. "I need to know if there's something we're missing—something that could explain why all this is happening."

Amos's face softened for a moment, a flicker of pain crossing his eyes. "Your mother was a wonderful woman. She loved you girls with all her heart. But she did have feelings for Herbert. It's true. And those rumors... they were spread by people who wanted to keep them apart."

"Who?" Ruthie pressed, stepping around the desk. "Who would do that?"

Amos looked away; his jaw clenched. "I don't know, Ruthie. It was a long time ago. People talked, and it caused a lot of pain. But your mother and I had a good life together. We made it work despite the rumors."

Ruthie's heart was heavy with the weight of her father's words. "I just want to understand, *Datt*."

Amos reached out, placing a rough hand on her shoulder.

"Sometimes, making things right means letting go of the past. Quit digging up the past and focus on the future, Ruthie. Your mother would want that."

Ruthie swallowed hard. "But *Datt*… I think that whoever caused so much trouble in the past may be the same person who is at the core of the break-ins and the hunt for this mysterious treasure."

Amos shook his head. "You just need to drop it."

"I don't think we can. Until the treasure is found, and we figure out who's responsible for these break-ins, the hunt for the treasure will keep on surfacing. Whatever Herbert buried for *Mamm* to find must be discovered to put an end to it all."

Amos walked to the door as someone hollered for him out in the mill. He stopped near the door and turned to Ruthie. "The past always has a way of catching up with people when they least expect it. This is getting out of hand. Please Ruthie, stopping dredging up the past before it's too late."

As Ruthie left the office, the sounds of the mill faded into the background, replaced by the whirlwind of thoughts in her mind. She knew her father was adamant about her letting the past stayed buried, but she was driven to uncover the truth—no matter how painful it might be.

CHAPTER 14

The day dawned gray and somber; the sky heavy with the promise of rain. Ruthie and Isaiah met at the bakery early in the morning, their expressions mirroring the tension that hung between them. They had agreed to review the clues once more, hoping to find something they had missed.

Isaiah spread the map and notes across the table, his brow furrowed in concentration. "We've gone over everything a hundred times, Ruthie. There's got to be something we're not seeing."

"I know. But we have to keep trying."

Just as they were about to delve deeper, the door to the bakery swung open, and a figure stepped inside. It was Evert, his face set in a determined scowl.

"Evert, what are you doing here?" Ruthie asked, her voice tinged with suspicion.

Evert approached the table, his eyes flicking between

Ruthie and Isaiah. "I've been watching Hilda. I saw my old friends visiting her, as well as Samuel Glick and Jedediah Weaver. It's odd that so many people are visiting her back door. It can only mean Hilda has something to gain by interacting with those men."

Ruthie and Isaiah exchanged a wary glance. "What else did you find out?" Isaiah asked.

Evert leaned in; his voice low. "I snooped around her farm when she wasn't home. Ruthie, did you know Hilda has an old car stored in the back of one of her barns?"

Ruthie's eyes widened in shock. "A car? What is she doing with a car?"

Evert's expression hardened. "I don't know, but it doesn't seem right."

Isaiah began, "First, we have the recipe box with the pinwheel design. Your mother's recipes were inside, and we're sure Hilda stole them. But who broke into the bakery? It had to be someone who knew you'd be away during the attempted bank break-in."

Ruthie continued, "Then, there's the engraved inscription I found in my mother's diary: '*In threads of old, the past does dwell. Find the book, the book that holds the tale.*' We're sure this clue points to the missing quilt ledger. And then there's the quilt my mother made for Herbert."

Isaiah nodded. "Next, we have the clue etched in the table at the buggy shop: '*Seek the harness that guides the way, where secrets lie, and history stays.*' That led us to *Noah's Harness Shop*, but why steal the map and leave the frame? The frame had an inscription on the back: '*The key you hold, the map's path shows, beneath the bench, treasures glow.*'"

Ruthie added, "And then the message carved into the bench: '*Where the pinwheel turns and shadows meet, go to the spot where secrets greet.*'"

Isaiah finished, "Finally, the clue from the safe deposit box: '*Where dawn breaks, the truth awaits. Behind tools rest, the path is best.*' And what about Hilda? How does she tie into all of this? We heard she might have once loved Herbert. Could she be the one who spread the rumors and caused so much havoc? Is she the one looking for the treasure?"

Evert's eyes darkened. "And what about the Old Mill? I took a ride out there and didn't see anything that would give us another clue."

Isaiah's expression turned grim. "And why break into my shop? It's all so confusing."

As the tension in the bakery reached its peak, the door opened once more, and two men strode in, their faces a mask of smug satisfaction.

"Well, well," the taller man said, his voice dripping with condescension. "Looks like we have ourselves a little standoff." Evert's eyes were wide. "What are you doing?"

The men's eyes glittered with malice. "We're here to make sure you don't get in the way. You've been a thorn in our side for too long, Evert."

Isaiah's jaw tightened. "You won't get away with this. The police are already involved."

The second man laughed, a harsh, grating sound. "The police? They don't know half of what's going on. And by the time they figure it out, it will be too late."

Evert stepped forward; his eyes blazing. "This has gone too far. You're putting everyone at risk."

The man's expression hardened. "Shut up, Evert. You're just as deep in this as we are. Don't pretend you're innocent. You want to find the treasure as badly as we do. You may have your friends here convinced, but you don't fool us."

Ruthie's mind raced. She needed to find a way out of this. She needed to go get help. But the odds seemed insurmountable.

As the men continued their threats, Ruthie's eyes darted around the room, searching for an escape route. Her eyes landed on the back door, slightly ajar.

She caught Isaiah's eye, nodding subtly toward the door. He understood immediately.

Without warning, Isaiah lunged at one of the men, knocking him off balance. "Run, Ruthie!" he shouted.

Ruthie didn't hesitate. She bolted for the back door with the sound of scuffling and shouting behind her.

She burst into the alley, the cool morning air hitting her face. Ruthie glanced back, her heart pounding. "I need to get help," she said, her voice breathless.

Ruthie burst into the police station, her heart pounding and her breath coming in short gasps. She didn't even notice the curious glances from the few people in the waiting area as she made a beeline for the front desk.

"Please, I need to see Detective Powers!" she demanded, her voice trembling with urgency.

The officer at the front desk, a young woman with a kind face, looked up from her computer. "Calm down, ma'am.

What's the emergency?"

Ruthie's words tumbled out in a rush. "There are men at my bakery. They threatened us. Detective Powers needs to know—"

At that moment, the door to the back office swung open, and Detective Powers appeared, leading Jedidiah in handcuffs. Ruthie's eyes widened in surprise at the sight of him.

"Detective Powers!" she called out, her voice rising with desperation.

Detective Powers looked up, his eyes narrowing as he recognized her. "Ruthie, what's going on?"

"There are men at my bakery threatening us. We think they're connected to the thefts and the treasure hunt. They're dangerous, Detective."

Detective Powers exchanged a glance with the officer at the desk before turning his attention to Jedidiah. "Take him to the interrogation room. I'll be there shortly."

The officer nodded, leading Jedidiah away as Detective Powers focused on Ruthie. "Tell me everything."

Ruthie tried to calm herself. "We've been piecing together clues about the treasure. Evert saw Samuel and two other men visiting Hilda Hiltey's bakery. They're all connected somehow.

We think Hilda is involved, and these men are trying to find the treasure first. They've threatened us."

Detective Powers listened intently, his expression growing more serious with each word. "And you think these men are at your bakery right now?"

With a respectful nod, Ruthie frantically added, "Yes, Isaiah tried to hold them off so I could get help. Please, Detective, you must do something."

Detective Powers didn't hesitate. He turned to the officer at the desk. "Call for backup and send units to the bakery immediately."

Ruthie felt a wave of relief wash over her as the officer began making calls. As they moved to a quieter corner of the station, Ruthie couldn't shake the image of Isaiah bravely confronting the men, allowing her to escape. She prayed silently that they would arrive in time and that Isaiah would be okay.

***

Hilda and Greta sat in the dimly lit kitchen of Hilda's old farmhouse. The rain outside pounded against the windows, adding to the tension in the room. Hilda was pacing back and forth, her frustration evident. Greta watched her *schwester's* movements with concern.

"You've been restless all evening. What's bothering you?" Greta asked, her voice soft.

Hilda stopped pacing and turned to Greta; her eyes filled with frustration. "It's Ruthie. She's digging into the past, asking questions about the quilt and the old stories. I'm certain she sent Martha to check out that old quilt on the wall. She's getting too close to the truth."

Greta frowned. "What truth? Why does it matter so much?"

Hilda tried to steady her emotions. "Because it all comes back to Herbert and Elsie. Ruthie's mother and I were close friends once. But Herbert only had eyes for Elsie. No matter what I did, he never noticed me."

Greta's eyes widened in surprise. "I didn't know you felt that way about Herbert."

Hilda's voice trembled. "I loved him. But he chose Elsie. My love turned to bitterness when I realized I could never have him. I spread rumors about them, trusting it would drive them apart. And it worked. Herbert was sent away, and Elsie married Amos."

Greta gasped. "You did that? You ruined their lives?"

Hilda's expression hardened. "I thought it would make me feel better, but it didn't. The betrayal I felt from Elsie cut deep. I wanted to prove I was better than her, that I could succeed where she failed. But her daughter's bakery is thriving while mine struggles."

Greta shook her head, tears in her eyes. "This obsession with the past is destroying you. Why can't you let it go?"

Hilda's eyes flashed with anger. "Because I need to reclaim what was taken from me. The treasure should have been for me, not Elsie. Stealing Ruthie's recipes and sabotaging her business is my way of getting back at Elsie."

Greta's voice was filled with fear. "Hilda, this is madness. You're risking everything for revenge."

Hilda clenched her fists, her voice cold. "I won't stop until I've secured my future. Ruthie's bakery will crumble, and I will find the treasure that is rightfully mine."

Greta's face paled. "But you're not the only one looking for the treasure. Others are just as desperate."

Hilda's lips curled into a bitter smile. "Let them try. I've waited too long for this moment. I won't let anyone stand in my way, not even Ruthie."

Greta reached out, grabbing her *schwester's* hand. "Please,

Hilda, think about what you're doing. This isn't just about you anymore."

Hilda pulled her hand away. "I know what I'm doing."

Greta's eyes filled with tears. "Our faith teaches us to forgive, to let go of grudges. Harboring so much bitterness will destroy you. It's not too late to make things right."

Hilda's expression softened for a moment before hardening again. "I can't forgive Elsie for stealing Herbert from me."

Greta wiped her tears and nose. "What about the two strange men, and why are you conspiring with Samuel and Jedidiah? What are you up to?"

"Those men are just a means to an end. They help me get what I need. As for Samuel and Jedidiah, they're too greedy to see they're being used. I promised them a share of the treasure."

Greta's voice was barely above a whisper. "This isn't right. This isn't how we were raised."

Hilda looked away as the rain continued to pour outside, mirroring the storm brewing within her.

Greta's voice broke the heavy silence. "Hilda, are you responsible for all the break-ins?"

"I can barely walk up the stairs, let alone ransack businesses. Of course not. But I have no idea what those I'm working with are capable of."

***

Rain poured down in sheets as Ruthie and Detective Powers hurried back to the bakery, their footsteps splashing through puddles on the way. The wind whipped around them, making the downpour even more intense. Ruthie's heart pounded in her chest as they approached the bakery, dread settling in her stomach.

As they reached the bakery, they saw the door wide open. A cold sense of fear washed over Ruthie. "Isaiah!" she called out, rushing inside.

Detective Powers followed close behind, his hand on his holstered weapon. They stopped short when they saw Isaiah lying unconscious on the floor, rainwater pooling around him. The clues and papers that had been on the table were missing.

Ruthie dropped to her knees beside Isaiah, shaking his shoulders gently. "Isaiah, wake up! Please, wake up."

Isaiah groaned, his eyes fluttering open. He winced, trying to sit up. "…what happened?"

Detective Powers knelt. "Isaiah, can you remember

anything? Where are Evert and the two men?"

Isaiah rubbed his head, wincing at the pain. "They jumped me. I don't know where they went."

Detective Powers helped Isaiah to his feet, his tone demanding but concerned. "What's Evert Miller's connection to all this?"

Isaiah steadied himself against the counter, taking a measured breath. "Evert's my cousin. We've been trying to get to the treasure to stop all this madness."

Ruthie added, "He used to live in Willow Springs, but his family moved to Willow Brook when we were kids. Evert was always a bit wild. As far as I know, he's been on the wrong side of the law more than once."

"I've been on Evert's trail myself, but I couldn't figure out his connection to the events here. With the two alleged bank robbers, things are falling into place."

Isaiah's face hardened. "Are you suggesting Evert used me to get to the treasure?"

Detective Powers shrugged. "It's a possibility. Do you think he would?"

Isaiah's eyes filled with disappointment. "I wouldn't put it past him, but I hoped he was trying to do the right thing this time. We were supposed to be working together to protect our families' legacies."

Isaiah took a deep breath, gathering his thoughts. "Evert mentioned that Hilda has an old car stored in one of her barns. He suspected she was hiding something there."

Detective Powers' eyes narrowed. "Is it an old blue Pontiac?"

Isaiah frowned, thinking back. "If it is, then that's the car I saw driving away from the bank."

Ruthie's eyes widened in shock. "Hilda's car? I knew she was involved somehow, but a bank robbery? That's a little much to believe even for Hilda."

"Can you remember anything else or know where they might be headed?"

"The letter we found in the safe deposit box mentions the old mill at dawn. I'm sure that's where they'll go next," Ruthie added.

Detective Powers checked his watch. "The clue says at dawn, so we have time. That gives me a chance to go question Hilda."

Detective Powers looked toward Isaiah. "Do you have any idea what this treasure might be?"

Isaiah shook his head. "I don't know. So many people are trying to find it. Who knows what will happen when it's discovered?"

Detective Powers' eyes narrowed. "Whatever it is, it's causing a lot of problems. We need to end this before someone else gets hurt."

As the rain continued to fall, they knew they had a long night ahead of them, but they were ready to face whatever came their way. Together, they would uncover the truth and bring peace back to Willow Springs.

Detective Powers turned to Ruthie. "By the way, I brought Jedidiah Weaver in for questioning."

Ruthie shook her head. "I saw him in handcuffs, but why?" Detective Powers replied, "We have him on film making a copy of a map at the drugstore. It looks like he printed it from a picture on a phone. I don't think he stole the map from Noah's harness shop, but it's suspicious that he would take a picture and make a copy."

Isaiah's eyes widened. "Evert mentioned seeing Jedidiah at Hilda's. That ties him to whatever she's up to."

Detective Powers nodded. "We need to piece all this together. If Hilda is involved, and Jedidiah is working with her, we might be able to find out more by questioning him."

CHAPTER 15

Isaiah paced his small apartment, the tension from the bakery still gnawing at him. He needed to clear his head and think, but his mind kept returning to the mysteries and secrets that seemed to be unraveling all at once. As he sat on the edge of his bed, something caught his eye—a corner of a brown package sticking out from behind the bedframe.

Suddenly, he remembered the package he had received weeks ago and had forgotten in all the chaos. He reached down and pulled it out, tearing off the paper wrapping. Inside, he found an old, leather-bound journal.

Curiosity piqued, Isaiah opened the journal, his fingers tracing the faded handwriting. It was his uncle Herbert's journal, a detailed account of his life and the many secrets he had kept. Each entry painted a clearer picture of the past.

Isaiah sat down at his small kitchen table; the journal open before him. The first few entries were mundane, detailing daily life and work. But as he flipped through the pages, he came across entries that sent chills down his spine.

July 5, 1980

Today, I carved another clue into the old bench across from the quilt shop. I hope Elsie finds it soon. It will guide her to the next step. I must be careful; Hilda is watching closely. She knows more than she lets on, and I know she saw us with the child.

August 15, 1980

Elsie and I met at the old mill. It's the only place I can find we won't be spotted.

September 10, 1980

The rumors are spreading. I can't believe the lies Hilda is telling. She's determined to come between Elsie and me. I fear for Elsie's safety and the secrets we've worked so hard to hide.

Isaiah's heart raced as he realized the journal's significance. Herbert had documented everything—the clues, the hiding places, and the threats from Hilda. He flipped to the last entry, dated just before Herbert was sent away.

October 2, 1980

I left Elsie a letter today. I pray she finds it and heeds my warning to follow the clues, find the treasure, and let our love guide her. Trust no one but your heart. We had to protect them, Elsie. Your brother and my sister needed us, and we couldn't let them be found. Hilda's lies were cruel, but they kept everyone's eyes on us and off them.

Isaiah looked at the clock, tucked the old journal into his pocket, and headed out into the rain. As the dark surrounded him, Isaiah tried to make sense of the secret and what it meant. He couldn't get to the Mast farm quickly enough.

Ruthie was quick to answer the door, and Isaiah stepped inside, shaking the rain from his hat.

Isaiah showed Ruthie the journal, his hands shaking slightly. "It wasn't just about them. They were protecting someone."

Ruthie read the entry. "My uncle… and your aunt? They ran away together?"

Isaiah replied, "And Herbert and Elsie took the blame.

Hilda's rumor tore their families apart." Isaiah handed her a letter that was never sent. "Read this."

Ruthie walked to the table, held the aged paper under the light, and read the entry out loud.

Elsie, my dearest,

The lies Hilda spreads are like poison, seeping into every corner of our lives. How could she stoop so low, painting you in such a vile light? You have always been my beacon of purity and grace. I would never dishonor you, never dream of doing anything that would jeopardize your reputation.

I'm certain Hilda saw you carrying my schwester's child and leapt to the worst conclusions. She doesn't know the truth: Your visit to your sick aunt gave Hilda the perfect opening to weave her deceitful tale.

She saw what she wanted to see and spun it into a web of lies, a web that now threatens to entangle us both.

Our love is strong, Elsie, stronger than her lies. We must stay true to each other and our promise. We will protect those we love, even if it means bearing the brunt of her cruel gossip.

One day, the truth will shine through, and the love we share will guide us to the treasure that symbolizes all we have fought for.

Forever yours,
Herbert

Ruthie took a deep breath, the weight of the revelation sinking in. "This is awful. My mother took the brunt of Hilda's jealousy with such grace."

Isaiah agreed, his determination matching hers. "And we need to stop Hilda. She's been pulling the strings for too long."

***

Isaiah and Ruthie sat at the table. The rain continued to patter against the windows, creating a rhythmic backdrop to their intense discussion. Spread out before them were Herbert's and Elsie's journals.

Isaiah looked up from the journal, his eyes meeting Ruthie's. "This last clue, '*Where dawn breaks, the truth awaits. Behind tools rest, the path is best.*' it's leading us to the old mill at dawn."

Ruthie's mind raced. "But what does it mean? What truth will be drawn?"

Isaiah leaned back, rubbing his temples. "It has to be something significant. Something that ties all these clues together."

Ruthie glanced down at the journal, her mother's handwriting staring back at her. "Maybe it's not just about the treasure. Maybe it's about uncovering the truth about our families. Maybe it's more about them causing a stir to keep the focus off my mother's brother."

Ruthie's face paled. "So, all of this... it's because of Hilda's jealousy?"

Isaiah nodded understandingly. "And now she's after the treasure. But we need to figure out what this final clue means."

Ruthie looked up at the clock. "Then we go to the old mill at dawn."

"But first, let's go into the attic. I'd love to look through some of my mother's diaries again. We might find the missing piece there."

Ruthie put her fingers on her lips as they moved through the kitchen to the attic door. Her father had gone to bed long ago, and she certainly didn't want to wake him since he wasn't happy about her digging up the past.

The attic was dimly lit, the only light coming from the old

kerosene lamp Ruthie had placed on a wooden crate. The air was thick with dust, and the musty smell of old books and forgotten memories filled the space. Ruthie and Isaiah sat on the floor, surrounded by stacks of her mother's diaries.

Ruthie held one of the diaries in her lap, her fingers tracing the worn leather cover. "There's so much I don't know about my mother's past."

Isaiah's eyes scanned the room. "Sometimes the past can hold the key to understanding the present. Let's see what else we can find."

Ruthie opened the diary and began to read aloud. The entries were filled with details about her mother's daily life, her hopes, and her dreams. As they read, they stumbled upon an entry that caught their attention.

May 12, 1979

I fear for my brother, Nathan. He's gotten himself into a mess again, and I don't know how to help him. He's always been a wild spirit, and now it seems he's fallen in with a bad crowd. Herbert has tried to talk some sense into him, but he doesn't listen to anyone.

Herbert's sister, Rebecca, is also in trouble. She's been

seen with some unsavory characters, and I worry about her. Herbert and I have tried to protect them, but it's hard when they don't want to be helped.

Ruthie's voice faltered as she read the words, her voice etched with emotion. "I had no idea my uncle Nathan was in so much trouble."

Isaiah leaned closer. "It sounds like your mother and Herbert were trying to keep their families out of trouble. Maybe that's part of the secret they were keeping."

Ruthie agreed. "It makes sense. If they were trying to protect Nathan and Rebecca, they would have kept it quiet. But why would Hilda spread rumors about my mother?"

"Hilda saw something and misunderstood it. Or maybe she spread the rumors on purpose to hurt your mother and Herbert."

Ruthie turned the page, her eyes scanning the next entry. "Let's see if there's more."

May 18, 1979

Nathan came to see me today. He's scared and doesn't know what to do. I promised him I would help, but I don't know how. Herbert is determined to protect Rebecca's reputation, but she's as stubborn as Nathan. They've both gotten in over their heads… and now a baby that they're not equipped to raise.

Herbert and I have decided to keep our relationship a secret for now. It's too dangerous with everything that's happening. I hate hiding our love, but it's the only way to keep everyone safe. I pray that one day, we can be together without fear.

Ruthie's voice broke as she read the words, the pain and fear her mother had felt echoing in her heart. "They were trying to protect their siblings. That's why they kept their relationship a secret."

Isaiah's face turned serious. "And it looks like Hilda's rumors were a way to drive them apart. If people believed the worst about your mother, it would ruin her reputation and force Herbert's family to step in."

Ruthie closed the diary, her hands trembling. "We need to find out more. If Nathan and Rebecca had a baby, where are they now?"

"We're getting closer to the truth, Ruthie. I feel it."

As they continued to search through the diaries, the pieces of the puzzle began to fall into place. The mystery of the hidden treasure and the secrets of the past were slowly being revealed, bringing Ruthie and Isaiah closer to understanding their families' true legacy.

Ruthie and Isaiah tiptoed around, careful not to disturb anything as they made their way back toward the steps.

Isaiah's clumsy self tripped over an uneven floorboard, causing him to stumble and knock over an old trunk. The lid flew open, and its contents spilled across the attic floor. Ruthie gasped, quickly bending down to pick up the scattered items.

"Isaiah, be quiet!" she whispered urgently, her eyes darting towards the attic stairs. "We don't want to wake up *Datt*."

"I'm sorry," Isaiah mumbled. He began chattering nervously, "I didn't mean to, I just—"

"Shhh!" Ruthie hissed, holding a finger to her lips.

As they gathered the spilled items, Ruthie couldn't believe what she was seeing. The scattered contents were the quilt ledger, a can of red paint, and a rolled-up map.

Isaiah's fingers fumbled with the quilt ledger, his hands shaking slightly. "Ruthie, these are... these are the missing clues that were stolen from the Quilt Market and Noah's Harness Shop." Isaiah held up a paint can. "This is the same color paint that was used on the side of my shop."

Ruthie's mind was a chaotic storm. "What are they doing

up here?"

Before Isaiah could respond, they heard a creak on the stairs. Ruthie's heart pounded as she saw her father standing at the top of the stairs, his face filled with dismay.

"*Datt...*" Ruthie began, her voice trembling. "How did these things find their way to the attic?"

Amos's shoulders sagged, and he looked down, unable to meet Ruthie's eyes. "I was trying to protect your mother's memory. I didn't want the past to be dug up and tarnish her name again."

Ruthie and Isaiah sat at the kitchen table with the ledger, the quilt, the map, and Amos's confession spread out before them. The flickering light and hiss from the kerosene lamp enhanced the mysterious atmosphere.

Ruthie traced her fingers over the old quilt journal they had found in the attic, her mind racing with the clues they had discovered. "*Where iron meets flame, secrets hide. Follow the forge, it's your guide,*" she read aloud, her voice barely above a whisper.

"That must be pointing to the old blacksmith shop," Isaiah said, his voice filled with certainty.

Ruthie gave a quick nod, her eyes scanning the ledger. "And

look here, it says that Herbert's quilt was sold to Susan Hiltey."

Amos, who had been sitting quietly in the corner, spoke up, his voice calm and resigned. "Susan Hiltey is Hilda's mother."

Ruthie exclaimed. "The quilt must be a clue. We need to go get it."

Isaiah, holding the ledger, paused and looked at Amos. "Why did you mess with my shop and leave that threatening message?"

Amos's face was etched with regret. "I just wanted you both to stop digging. I figured if I had a few of the clues, you'd never be able to complete the puzzle and find the treasure. I've lived with the pain of not being Elsie's first love all my life. I just wanted the past to stay buried. I didn't want Ruthie to discover the extent of what her mother was being accused of."

Ruthie's heart ached for her father, but she couldn't ignore the importance of the clues they had uncovered. "*Datt*, I understand why you did it, but we need to see this through. It's not just about the treasure; it's about finding the truth and clearing *Mamm's* name."

Isaiah gave a slight nod in agreement. "We're so close. We can't stop now."

The resolve in Ruthie's voice was unmistakable. She and

Isaiah were determined to follow the clues and uncover the truth, no matter where it led them. The past may have been buried, but it was time to bring it into the light and find closure for the pain that had haunted their families for so long.

***

In the dark of the night, Ruthie and Isaiah hitched the buggy and made their way to Hilda's farm. The cool air was filled with tension and anticipation. As they approached, the flickering lights of police cars illuminated the scene. Detective Powers was already there, a search warrant in hand, directing officers to search Hilda's barn.

Isaiah tied the buggy to the hitching post, and they walked up the porch steps. Just as they reached the door, they saw Detective Powers leading Hilda to the police car, her face a mask of bitter resignation.

Greta stood on the porch, tears streaming down her face. "I tried to talk sense into her, but she wouldn't listen. She's been filled with resentment for so long. It ate away at her good judgment all her life."

Ruthie approached Greta, placing a comforting hand on her

shoulder. "Greta, I'm so sorry. But we need the quilt. It's important."

Greta looked confused. "Why would you want my mother's old quilt?"

Ruthie glanced at Isaiah before answering. "It's part of a series of clues we've been following. It's tied to our families' past and a treasure that's been hidden for years."

Greta bobbed her head slowly, leading them into the bakery. As they entered, Ruthie's eyes immediately fell on the quilt hanging on the wall. The pinwheel design matched that of her recipe box and the quilt ledger. But the center block caught her attention—a single windmill, just like the one near her father's sawmill.

Isaiah stepped closer, examining the quilt. "This is it. This is the final piece of the puzzle."

Ruthie reached out, her fingers gently tracing the windmill design. "My mother made this for Herbert. It's the key to everything."

Greta watched them, her expression one of bewilderment and sorrow. "I never understood why Hilda held onto it for so long. It was like she couldn't let go of the past."

Ruthie turned to Greta; her eyes filled with empathy.

"Hilda's actions were driven by pain and jealousy. But we're here to find the truth and bring closure to our families."

Detective Powers walked back into the bakery, his eyes meeting Ruthie's. "We found the car, and it matches the description of the one used in the bank robbery. Hilda's going to have a lot to answer for."

Ruthie nodded affirmatively, a sense of relief washing over her. "Thank you, Detective. We couldn't have done this without you."

Isaiah took Ruthie's hand, squeezing it gently. "We're almost there, Ruthie. We'll find the treasure and the truth."

Together, they stood in the bakery, surrounded by the remnants of Hilda's bitterness, but united in their quest for the truth. The quilt, with its intricate designs and hidden meanings, was the key to unraveling the mystery that had haunted their families for so long. And with each step, they were closer to uncovering the secrets that had been buried for decades.

CHAPTER 16

The predawn air was crisp and cool as Ruthie and Isaiah made their way to the old mill, their buggy rumbling softly along the dirt path. The rain had long stopped, and the clouds were clearing, revealing a sky dotted with the first hints of morning light.

Isaiah, unable to contain his excitement, chattered incessantly. "You know, Ruthie, this reminds me of when I tried to solve the mystery of the missing tools at my *datt's* shop. I couldn't sit still then, either. My *datt* always said my brain worked like a whirlwind."

Ruthie's heart warmed at his constant noise. She had grown fond of his quirks, finding comfort in his unique mannerisms. "I think your brain is a wonderful whirlwind. I hardly notice you playing with your collar anymore. It's become a part of you, just like your constant interrupting."

Isaiah looked at her, his eyes sparkling with affection. "And your no-nonsense attitude and bossy ways are two of the reasons we get along so well. You keep me grounded."

She chuckled softly. "We balance each other out. I never thought I'd find someone who could put up with me."

As they approached the mill, the structure loomed against the slowly brightening sky, its old wooden beams creaking softly in the morning breeze. They arrived a few minutes before dawn, just as the first light began to touch the horizon.

Isaiah helped Ruthie down from the buggy, his hands lingering on hers for a moment longer than necessary. They walked together towards the mill, their steps echoing in the stillness.

Isaiah's voice softened as they approached the entrance. "We have the map, the quilt, the ledger, and all the clues we've gathered have led us here. This is it, I'm sure of it."

Ruthie nodded briefly, her heart pounding with anticipation. *"Where dawn breaks, the truth awaits,"* she whispered, recalling the final clue.

Isaiah's fingers fidgeted with the edge of the map as they entered the mill. The old structure creaked and groaned; its history evident in the air. They laid out the quilt, the ledger, and the map on an old workbench, each piece fitting together like a puzzle.

They walked through the old building, eyes scanning the scattered array of old tools on the workbench, the grinding stone, and the antique boxes and implements long forgotten.

Isaiah kept repeating, *"Behind tools rest, the path is best."* They moved towards the grinding stone platform, and together they pointed to the tool chest pushed up against the wall, wondering if those were the tools the clues referred to. Just as Isaiah started looking through the old toolbox, Ruthie spotted a small hole burrowed in the wall just above the chest.

"Move the box," Ruthie urged. As they shifted the chest, light from the rising sun began to filter through the mill, illuminating the wall. Suddenly, as the first hint of light lifted above the horizon, a beam poured in, highlighting an outline of the pinwheel design. Someone had meticulously burrowed holes in the old wall in the shape of the pinwheel design, with one point pointing off to one side.

They followed the design to the window on the far side of the building. They both gasped as the design pointed out the window to the windmill in the field on the other side of the mill.

Just then, Evert was pushed through the door and fell at their feet, with the two men on his heels. One of them, tall and menacing, stepped forward and grabbed Isaiah by the collar. "Hand over the rest of the clues," he growled, shaking Isaiah.

The other man yanked Ruthie towards the workbench, his grip tightening around her arm. "You better start talking, or things are going to get really bad," he snarled.

Isaiah's heart pounded as he saw the fear in Ruthie's eyes. "Let her go," he said, his voice trembling but determined. "We'll tell you what you want to know, just don't hurt her."

Evert, struggling to his feet, tried to reason with them. "We're all after the same thing. There's no need for threats."

"Shut up!" one of the men barked, shoving Evert back down. "You had your chance to talk. Now it's her turn."

Ruthie's mind raced as she tried to piece together everything they had learned. "The pinwheel design points to the windmill," she said, her voice quavering. "That's where we need to go next."

The man holding her sneered, tightening his grip. "Good," he hissed. "You're coming with us to ensure you're not lying."

Isaiah's eyes darted around the room, desperate for a way out. "Look," he said quickly, pointing to the design, "it's all there. Just let Ruthie go."

The second man laughed, a cold, cruel sound. "You think we're stupid? You're coming with us too. Both of you."

The man shoved Ruthie towards the door. "No more talking. Move it." Squeezing Ruthie's arm harder, he continued, "And you… grab that shovel. We're going to need it."

Isaiah's mind raced, his hands shaking as he took the shovel from the hook on the wall. He couldn't let anything happen to Ruthie. As they were forced towards the exit, he glanced at Ruthie, their eyes locking. A silent promise passed between them: They would find a way out of this together.

They stepped outside, the cool air hitting their faces. The path to the windmill stretched out before them, and with it, the uncertain fate that awaited them all.

Ruthie and Isaiah, accompanied by the two men and Evert, approached the structure's base, each step toward the windmill heavy with unspoken dread.

The two men kept a close eye on Isaiah as they started to dig at the base of the windmill. The sound of the shovel biting into the earth seemed to echo louder than it should have. Ruthie's heart raced with each passing second.

Finally, the shovel hit something solid. Isaiah and Evert

exchanged a glance, and together they pulled a weathered metal box from the ground. It was old; the metal darkened with age and moisture, but intact.

One of the men reached forward, yanking the box from their hands. He fumbled with the latch; his impatience evident when he found it was locked.

The other man wrenched the key out of Ruthie's hand and threw it at the man on the ground. He threw the lid open when the key finally gave way, expecting to see glittering treasure. Instead, his face twisted in confusion.

"What is this?" he snarled, pulling out a stack of yellowed letters and documents.

Ruthie leaned over, her breath catching as she recognized the handwriting. "These are letters from Herbert and Elsie," she whispered.

The men looked at each other, bewildered. Just then, Detective Powers stepped out of the shadows, flanked by several officers. "You're both under arrest for attempted burglary, kidnapping, and conspiracy," he declared, his voice firm.

"Get them!" one of the men shouted, and suddenly, chaos erupted. The two men lunged at the officers, trying to make a run for it.

Evert and Isaiah sprang into action, rushing to help the officers contain the two men. Evert tackled one of them to the ground, struggling to keep him down as the man fought back fiercely. Isaiah, despite his usual nervous demeanor, managed to pin the other man against the windmill, holding him there until an officer could secure the handcuffs.

Ruthie watched in shock as the scuffle unfolded, her heart pounding in her chest. The scene was a blur of movement and shouts, but within moments, the officers had regained control. Both men were handcuffed, still cursing and struggling.

Detective Powers approached them, his eyes gleaming in the early light. "Hilda spilled everything. Your involvement is no secret anymore," he said to the men, his voice cold and authoritative.

The officers led them away. Evert, Ruthie, and Isaiah were left standing by the windmill, the box of secrets still in their hands.

Ruthie carefully unfolded one of the documents, her eyes scanning the pages. "This states that the child my mother's *bruder* and Herbert's *schwester* had was raised by Evert's grandparents," she said softly. She turned to Evert; her eyes wide with realization. "Evert… you're the child born out of wedlock."

Evert's face went pale, his hands trembling as he took the records from Ruthie. "I… I never knew," he stammered. "All this time, I never knew."

Isaiah reached into the box, pulling out a rolled-up deed. He unrolled it carefully, revealing a piece of valuable land. "This deed was meant to be a wedding gift from Herbert to Elsie," he explained.

Ruthie pulled out the final item in the box—a heartfelt letter from Herbert to Elsie. She read it aloud, her voice breaking with emotion.

My Dearest Elsie,

Our love for solving mysteries was one of the many joys we shared. Each clue, each little game, brought us closer together, and I cherished every moment we spent unraveling secrets. I crafted this treasure hunt with the hope that it would lead you to me, a testament of our bond and the adventures we loved.

Life, however, had different plans for us. Though we couldn't be together, I hope that this treasure finds its way into the hands of the child we fought so hard to protect. May he cherish it as much as we would have.

The land I leave is a token of my enduring love for you and my wish for peace and reconciliation between our families. May this gift bring them together, heal the wounds of the past, and allow them to enjoy life's mysteries and treasures.

Yours always, Herbert

As Ruthie finished reading, a profound silence fell over them. The weight of the past, the secrets, and the sacrifices made by Herbert and Elsie hung in the air. Evert looked at the birth records, then at Ruthie and Isaiah. "I spent so long searching for treasure, never realizing the true treasure was understanding what my family went through."

Giving a nod, Isaiah placed a comforting hand on Ruthie's shoulder. "This is more valuable than any gold or jewels. It's the truth and a way to put the rumors surrounding your mother finally to rest."

Ruthie smiled, feeling a sense of closure. "Herbert and Elsie's love story may have been tragic, but it brought us here, to this moment of truth and reconciliation. We can finally honor their memory by mending the rift between our families."

276

CHAPTER 17

Ruthie was busy arranging a new batch of fried pies when the doorbell chimed, signaling a customer. She looked up, expecting to see a regular, but was surprised to find Greta standing hesitantly at the entrance.

Greta walked slowly towards the counter; her expression somber. She reached into her bag and pulled out Ruthie's *mamma's* recipe box and cards, placing them gently on the counter. "I came to return these," she said softly.

Ruthie picked up the familiar box. "Thank you, Greta," she said, her voice filled with emotion. "I've missed these so much."

With an exasperated sigh, Greta's gaze dropped to the floor. "I also came to apologize for Hilda. Her jealousy, anger, and bitterness toward your mother ate away at her better judgment. She was never quite right after Herbert chose Elsie over her."

With a knowing nod, Ruthie remembered the stories and the pain that jealousy had caused.

Greta continued, her voice trembling slightly. "Hilda spread terrible rumors about your mother, claiming that it was she who had a child out of wedlock. For years, she believed that your older *schwester* was really Herbert's child. But Herbert wasn't like that. He'd never dishonor a woman in that way. It was Hilda's way of causing strife between the two families."

Ruthie listened intently. "It must have been so hard for you, Greta, living with all that bitterness."

Greta gave a nod of resolution, tears welling up in her eyes. "It was. Hilda's obsession with Herbert and her resentment towards your mother poisoned her heart. I tried to talk sense into her, but she was too consumed by her own pain."

She paused, taking a deep breath before continuing. "Despite all the rumors and the hurtful lies, your father still married your mother. He stood by her side, ignoring the gossip and choosing love over malicious words. That was a truly honorable thing to do, and it showed the depth of his character."

Ruthie's eyes softened, and she felt a new wave of respect for her father. "He did. He always loved her, no matter what."

Greta smiled through her tears. "It was a rare and beautiful thing, their love. Your father's strength and your mother's grace were inspiring. They showed that love can overcome even the most painful obstacles."

Ruthie reached across the counter and took Greta's hand. "I'm sorry for what you've been through. And I'm sorry for what Hilda did. But thank you for bringing these recipes back. You've returned a part of my mother I thought was lost forever."

Greta squeezed Ruthie's hand, a small smile breaking through her tears. "I hope this can be a new beginning for you. It's time to heal the wounds of the past and move forward."

Understandingly, Ruthie nodded, "*Jah*, it's time. Thank you, Greta."

As Greta left the bakery, Ruthie looked through her recipes, pulling the box close to her heart, hoping to sense her mother in the handwritten notes.

Later, Ruthie and Isaiah were enjoying a quiet afternoon in the bakery, the comforting hum of the oven filling the air with the scent of brewed coffee. They had just sat down with a cup of coffee when the doorbell tinkled, and Detective Powers stepped in, his expression serious.

"Detective Powers," Ruthie greeted him, standing up. "What brings you here?"

Detective Powers took off his hat and approached them, his eyes scanning the cozy interior of the bakery. "I have some updates regarding the investigation," he said, his voice grave. "We've brought Samuel in for questioning."

Ruthie's eyes got wide. "Samuel? What for?"

"Samuel has been implicated in the break-in at your bakery and the conspiracy involving Hilda," Detective Powers explained. "It turns out Hilda made some big promises to Jedidiah, Samuel, and the two men from Evert's past, claiming she knew more about the hidden treasure than she actually did. She is a bitter woman with no remorse for dragging these men into her schemes."

Isaiah exchanged a look with Ruthie, his glare troubled. "So, Hilda was behind everything?"

With a firm nod, Detective Powers agreed. "Yes, and no. She manipulated everyone around her, using their greed and desperation to further her own goals. She believed that finding the treasure would give her the validation and power she craved. But it was all based on lies and rumors. But only part of it, not all of it."

Ruthie felt a wave of relief but also sadness for the lengths to which Hilda had gone. "And Samuel?"

"We have enough evidence to suggest that Samuel was complicit in the break-in at your bakery," Detective Powers continued. "He was motivated by greed and the promise of a share in the treasure. But Hilda also manipulated him, by convincing him that the treasure was real and within their reach."

Ruthie leaned back in her chair, shaking her head. "It's hard to believe Samuel would get involved in something like this. I always knew he was ambitious, but this..."

"There's more," Detective Powers said, pulling out a file. "I did some digging into Eleanor Fischer. The land Evert Miller bought at a tax sale once belonged to her family. She was committed to reclaiming what she thought had been stolen from her."

Ruthie gasped. "So, Eleanor's involvement wasn't just about the treasure. She believed the land rightfully belonged to her. And get this, those two men are Eleanor's brothers. It seems that they've been up to no good for a good long time."

"Exactly," Detective Powers confirmed. "Eleanor's family lost the land due to unpaid taxes, and when she discovered that

Herbert had purchased it, she saw it as an opportunity to reclaim her family's legacy. She was willing to go to great lengths to get it back, and she felt the treasure was a way to claim what she felt was hers."

Isaiah frowned. "What will happen to her?"

"We're still investigating her involvement," Detective Powers said. "But for now, the focus is on bringing those directly involved to justice."

Ruthie sighed, feeling a mix of emotions. "It's so sad that all this happened because of greed and bitterness."

Detective Powers hesitated for a moment before continuing. "We still don't know who stole the ledger and the map or who vandalized your buggy shop, Isaiah. However, Noah and the Hostetler's have decided to drop the charges since the items have been returned. Isaiah, do you want to file any charges on the damage to your shop?"

Isaiah and Ruthie exchanged a quick glance. They both knew that Ruthie's father was trying to protect her mother's reputation. Isaiah shook his head. "No, I don't think that will be necessary."

The detective looked relieved. "That simplifies things. Thank you for your understanding."

With that, he left the bakery, the doorbell chiming softly as it closed behind him. Ruthie and Isaiah stood in silence for a moment, the weight of the encounter settled around them.

Isaiah broke the silence, his voice gentle. "Are you okay?" Ruthie's fingers still clutched the recipe box. "I think so. It's just… a lot to take in."

Ruthie walked to the window, pulled the shades, flipped the sign over, and locked the door. The last couple of days had drained every ounce of energy she had left, and she slumped down in a chair under the window.

Isaiah moved to sit across from her, watching her with concern. "You know, Ruthie, I've been thinking a lot about the future. About our future."

Ruthie looked up, her tired eyes meeting his. "Our future?" With a knowing nod, Isaiah continued fidgeting with the edge of the tablecloth. "Yeah. I mean, we've been through so much together. And I've come to realize that... I really care about you."

Ruthie smiled softly, a warm feeling spreading in her chest. "I care about you too. But you know I'm not exactly a typical Amish girl. I'm bossy, and I speak my mind. Can you really handle that?"

Isaiah chuckled, his nervous fingers still playing with the tablecloth. "Ruthie, I wouldn't want you any other way. And honestly, I need someone who can keep me grounded, who doesn't mind my oddness."

Ruthie's smile widened. "You really mean that?"

Isaiah nodded. "Absolutely. I've never met anyone like you, and I don't think I ever will again. I enjoy your bossiness and honesty. It's refreshing."

Ruthie laughed, a sound that was music to Isaiah's ears. "Well, you're certainly unique too. Your quirks, your constant need to move and talk, it's part of who you are. And I've come to find it endearing."

Isaiah's face lit up with relief and happiness. "So, does that mean we have a future together?"

Ruthie reached across the table, taking his fidgeting hands in hers. "I think we do."

Isaiah squeezed her hands gently. The two of them sat in comfortable silence for a moment, the weight of the past days slowly lifting. The storm outside had passed, leaving a sense of calm and clarity in its wake.

Ruthie took a deep breath, looking into Isaiah's eyes. "So, what do we do now?"

Isaiah grinned. "Well, I think we continue building our own paths. You have your bakery, and I have my buggy shop. But maybe, along the way, we can support each other, help each other grow."

Ruthie smiled. "I like the sound of that."

As they sat there, planning and dreaming about the days to come, Ruthie couldn't help but feel grateful for the journey that had brought them together. Despite all the challenges and mysteries, they had found something truly special in each other.

EPILOGUE

The air was filled with a sense of closure and new beginnings as Ruthie, Isaiah, and Evert stood together, ready to bury the metal box that held the letters, clues, and memories of a love long past.

Ruthie looked around at the faces of those she had come to care for deeply. Isaiah, fidgeting, stood determinedly, ready to honor the past and move forward. Evert looked sure as he finally understood the feeling of unrest that had plagued his childhood.

Isaiah cleared his throat, breaking the silence. "We're here to put the past to rest, to honor the love and sacrifices of those who came before us." He held up the metal box, its weight symbolic of the burdens they had all carried.

Ruthie stepped forward, her voice steady. "Let the past be only a distant memory and may our families always be joined by brotherly love."

With a respectful nod, Evert's eyes meet each of theirs in turn. "We've all made mistakes, but we've also found forgiveness and a chance to start anew. This box holds the past, but it's also a reminder of how secrets and rumors can ruin a family."

Together, they dug a small hole at the base of the windmill, the very place where the final clue had led them. As they lowered the metal box into the ground, Isaiah spoke softly. "The Bible teaches us to love thy neighbor as thyself," he said. "Holding onto bitterness and grudges only separates us from *Gott's* love."

As they covered the box with soil, each felt a sense of peace and closure. The past had been honored, and the lessons learned would guide them in the coming days.

Evert stepped forward, holding a deed in his hand. "This land was left to me, and it sits on the hill overlooking the windmill. As long as I live, I will know the importance of the windmill to our family's history."

He handed the deed to Isaiah and Ruthie. "I'm on a quest to find my biological parents. For the time being, I leave this land in your hands to build your future on. When and if I return, I will also make it my home."

Ruthie looked at the deed in her hands, feeling the weight of Evert's trust. "Thank you, Evert. We will take good care of it."

Isaiah nodded in agreement. "This land will symbolize our new beginning, a place where old grudges are buried, and love and forgiveness thrive."

As the sun climbed higher in the sky, they stood together, feeling the promise of a new day. The windmill creaked softly in the breeze, a silent witness to their moment of reconciliation and hope.

Ruthie stepped forward, her eyes reflecting the determination and faith she had inherited from her mother. "I hope my character can match that of my mother's. She will always stand as a beacon of what a good follower of Christ looks like. To lay her life down for others, no matter the cost."

They stood together in a circle, feeling the warmth of family and the power of forgiveness. The past was finally at rest, and the future stretched out before them, filled with promise and hope.

***

Read the next book in the Willow Springs Amish Mystery Romance series. - ***The Amish Widow's Last Stitch.***

After Widow Yoder's unexpected collapse, Lizzie can't shake the feeling that something is wrong. As mysterious clues begin to surface, Lizzie is determined to uncover the truth behind her grandmother's death.

The Amish

Widow's Last Stitch

A WILLOW SPRINGS
AMISH MYSTERY ROMANCE

Book 3

Tracy Fredrychowski

PROLOGUE

**Tragedy Strikes Willow Springs:
Beloved Yarn Shop Owner Dies Suddenly**
by Jonas Butler - The Buggy Crossing

Willow Springs, PA - The peaceful town of Willow Springs was shaken yesterday by the sudden death of one of its most cherished Main Street merchants, Widow Esther Yoder, owner of Simply Yarn. Widow Yoder collapsed while dining with her granddaughter, Lizzie Yoder, during a lunch break at The Restaurant on the Corner. She was 72.

Widow Yoder was a well-loved figure in the community, known for her gentle smile and the warm atmosphere of her yarn shop, which she ran with Lizzie. Simply Yarn had become a cornerstone of Main Street, attracting both Amish and English customers who enjoyed her skillful crochet work and her generous spirit.

As the community mourns the loss of one

of their most beloved members, many are left wondering if there is more to this tragedy than meets the eye. Simply Yarn will remain closed as Lizzie grieves and considers her future, but the shadow of suspicion now hangs over what once seemed like a peaceful passing.

A private memorial service will be held by her family and the New Order Amish Church. Bishop Schrock has asked the community to respect the family's privacy during this time of grief.

CHAPTER 1

The crisp autumn air drifted into The Restaurant on the Corner, carrying with it the earthy scent of fallen leaves and the faint aroma of wood smoke. Outside, the gentle clop of horse hooves and the soft creak of buggy wheels passing by added to the seasonal symphony. Main Street merchants, taking a break from their busy morning, filled the restaurant with a lively hum of conversation.

Widow Yoder, a cherished member of the Willow Springs community, sat by the window, savoring her usual bowl of chicken and dumplings. Beside her sat her granddaughter, Lizzie, her bright eyes filled with the joy of spending time with her beloved grandmother. They were on a lunch break from running Simply Yarn, their cozy shop that was as much a part of their lives as breathing. The familiar clinking of cutlery and the murmur of diners provided a comforting backdrop. Widow Yoder's crochet bag, a constant companion, rested at her feet, filled with yarn for her latest project.

"Lizzie, dear, you need to find someone who makes you as happy as this yarn shop does," Lizzie's grandmother said, her voice gentle yet firm. "David Hershberger seems like a nice young man."

Lizzie blushed, looking down at her half-eaten plate. "*Ach, Grossmommi,* I'm too busy with the shop to think about such things."

Her grandmother took a sip of her tea and frowned slightly. "This tea tastes a bit off today," she remarked, setting the cup down. She glanced out the window, her eyes distant and thoughtful.

Before Lizzie could respond, a sudden gasp cut through the chatter. The older woman's face contorted in pain; her hand clutched at her chest. She collapsed forward, her face landing in her bowl with a splash that sent broth across the table. Lizzie screamed, her voice piercing the air. For a moment, the restaurant was eerily silent, the only sound was the faint rustle of leaves outside the window.

Chaos erupted as patrons rushed to help, their movements frantic and disjointed. Lizzie knelt by her grandmother's side, her hands trembling as she tried to rouse her. Amidst the commotion, a nearby diner rose hurriedly, muttering about a forgotten appointment as he exited the restaurant. Another patron, with an oddly intense concern, began clearing the table with a nervous energy, his actions almost too eager.

Widow Yoder's crochet bag tipped over, its contents—balls of yarn and crochet hooks—scattering across the floor. The table settings were knocked askew, the faint residue in a teacup going unnoticed. A glassy object rolled quietly under the table, lost amid the scattered yarn and hooks. A crumpled piece of paper fluttered from her lap, quickly becoming part of the floor's clutter during the commotion.

As the staff and patrons worked together to call for help and tend to Widow Yoder, the autumn sounds continued to flow through the open window, a stark contrast to the shock inside. The beloved Widow had breathed her last, leaving behind a ripple of unease that spread through the restaurant. Lizzie clutched her grandmother's hand, her tears mingling with the broth on the table, her heart heavy with grief and confusion.

The whispers began almost immediately. Willow Springs was a place where everyone knew each other, where the most scandalous event was a runaway cow. A heart attack or stroke seemed the most likely cause. The Amish community believed that if it was God's will for someone to die, so be it. There would be no coroner's examination, no autopsy. Yet doubt lingered in Lizzie's mind.

In the weeks leading up to this day, Lizzie had observed strange things happening at the yarn shop. Items were misplaced, a few small amounts of money were missing, and once, she had found her grandmother reading something hurriedly, only to hide it as Lizzie approached. Her grandmother had been acting oddly, distracted, and more secretive than usual.

Something was unsettling about her grandmother's untimely death. Lizzie's suspicions grew. This wasn't just an unfortunate event; something was terribly wrong. The quiet, hidden clues would soon draw her into a web of mystery, challenging the very fabric of her peaceful existence. And at the heart of it all was the question: Who could possibly want to harm her *grossmommi*? And for Lizzie, another question loomed: How could she find the strength to face this tragedy and the courage to run Simply Yarn by herself?

***

Read the next book in the Willow Springs Amish Mystery Romance series. - ***The Amish Widow's Last Stitch.***

Lizzie Yoder can't ignore the strange events leading up to her grandmother's sudden death. As whispers of foul play grow, Lizzie must unravel the mystery before it unravels her.

RUTHIE'S FAMOUS LEMON FRY PIES

Fry Pie Dough:

Ingredients:

- 7 cups all-purpose flour
- 1 ½ tsp baking powder
- 2 tsp salt
- 2 tsp sugar
- 1 ½ cups shortening
- 2 eggs, beaten
- 1 ½ cup evaporated milk

Instructions:

1. In a large bowl, whisk together the flour, baking powder, salt, and sugar.

2. Add the shortening and use a pastry blender or fork to cut it into the dry ingredients until the mixture resembles coarse crumbs. It's fine to have some pea-sized bits remaining.

3. In a separate bowl, whisk together the beaten eggs and evaporated milk. Gradually add this to the flour mixture, stirring gently just until the dough comes together. Be careful not to overmix.

4. Roll the dough into 2 - 2 ½ inch balls and flatten each

into a 6 ½ inch circle. Use a 6-inch round object to cut out uniform circles.

5. Add about ⅓ cup of your chosen pie filling to one side of each circle. Moisten the edges with water, fold the other half over the filling, and press the edges together with a fork to seal.

6. Place the pies on a parchment-lined baking sheet and refrigerate them as you continue working to keep them cool. This recipe yields approximately 20 fry pies.

Frying:

1. Heat oil (canola or peanut oil) to 350°F in a deep fryer or large, heavy pot.

2. Fry the pies in small batches, about 3 minutes per side, or until golden brown. Flip halfway through to ensure even cooking.

3. Remove from the oil using a slotted spoon, and transfer to a wire rack to cool slightly.

Glaze:

Ingredients:

- 2 cups powdered sugar
- 1 tsp vanilla extract
- 4 tbsp milk

Instructions:

1. Whisk together the powdered sugar, vanilla, and milk until smooth.

2. Drizzle the glaze over the warm fry pies. Prepare the glaze just before you're ready to use it, as it thickens over time.

Storage:

- Store fry pies loosely covered in the fridge for up to 5 days.

- For longer storage, allow them to cool completely, then freeze in an airtight container. Thaw at room temperature before serving.

Baking Option:

For a healthier option, preheat your oven to 425°F. Cut a small slit in the top of each pie for venting. Bake for about 15 minutes or until golden brown.

Lemon Filling:

Ingredients:

- ¾ cup sugar
- 2 tbsp cornstarch
- ½ tsp salt

- ¾ cup water
- 2 slightly beaten egg yolks
- 3 tbsp lemon juice
- 1 tsp grated lemon peel
- 2 drops lemon oil (food-safe)
- 1 tbsp butter

Instructions:

1. In a medium saucepan, combine sugar, cornstarch, and salt.
2. Gradually stir in water, egg yolks, and lemon juice.
3. Cook over medium heat, stirring constantly, until the mixture thickens and begins to bubble.
4. Remove from heat and stir in the grated lemon peel, lemon oil, and butter until smooth.
5. Allow the filling to cool before using it in your fry pies.

Enjoy your delicious fry pies with this tangy lemon filling or any other favorite filling!

WHAT DID YOU THINK?

First of all, thank you for purchasing *The Amish Baker Caper – A Willow Springs Mystery Romance*. I hope you will enjoy all the books in this series.

You could have picked any number of books to read, but you chose this book, and for that, I am incredibly grateful. I hope it added value and quality to your everyday life. If so, it would be nice to share this book with your friends and family on social media.

If you enjoyed this book and found some benefit in reading it, I'd like to hear from you and hope that you would take some time to post a review on Amazon. Your feedback and support will help me improve my writing craft for future projects.

If you loved visiting Willow Springs, I invite you to sign up for my private email list, where you'll get to explore more of the characters of this Amish Community.

Sign up at https://dl.bookfunnel.com/v9wmnj7kve and download the novella that starts this series, *The Amish Women of Lawrence County*.

GLOSSARY
Pennsylvania Dutch "Deutsch" Words

Ausbund. Amish songbook.

bruder. B, but she didn't utter dad.

denki. Thank You.

doddi. Grandfather.

doddi house. A small house next to the main house.

g'may. Community

goot meiya. Good morning.

jah. Yes.

kapp. Covering or prayer cap.

kinner. Children.

mamm. Mother or mom.

mommi. Grandmother.

nee. No.

Ordnung. Order or set of rules the Amish follow.

rumshpringa. Running around period.

schwester. Sister.

singeon. Singing/youth gathering.

The Amish are a religious group typically referred to as Pennsylvania Dutch, Pennsylvania Germans, or Pennsylvania Deutsch. They are descendants of early German immigrants to Pennsylvania and their beliefs center around living a conservative lifestyle. They arrived between the late 1600s and the early 1800s to escape religious persecutions in Europe. They first settled in Pennsylvania with the promise of religious freedom by William Penn. Most Pennsylvania Dutch still speak a variation of their original German language as well as English.

ABOUT THE AUTHOR

Tracy Fredrychowski's life closely mirrors the gentle, simple stories she crafts in her writing. With a passion for the simpler side of life, Tracy regularly shares tips on her website and blog at tracyfredrychowski.com.

In northwestern Pennsylvania, Tracy grew up steeped in the virtues of country living. A pivotal moment in her life was the tragic murder of a young Amish woman in her community. This event profoundly influenced her, compelling her to dedicate her writing to the peaceful lives of the Amish people. Tracy aims to inspire her readers through her stories to embrace a life centered around faith, family, and community.

For those intrigued by the Amish way of life, Tracy extends an invitation to connect with her on Facebook. On her page and group, she shares captivating Amish photography by her friend Jim Fischer and recipes, short stories, and glimpses into her cherished Amish community nestled deep in the heart of northwestern Pennsylvania's Amish County.

Facebook.com/tracyfredrychowskiauthor/

Facebook.com/groups/tracyfredrychowski/